THREE DIRTY HARTS

A DIRTY NOVELLA

CARA DEE

THREE *Dirty* HARTS

Edited by Silently Correcting Your Grammar, LLC.
Formatting by Eliza Rae Services.

THE *Dirty* SERIES IN CAMASSIA COVE

Camassia Cove is a town in northern Washington created to be the home of some exciting love stories. Each novel taking place here is a standalone, with the exception of sequels, and they will vary in genre and pairing. What they all have in common is the town in which they live. Some are friends and family. Others are complete strangers. Some have vastly different backgrounds. Some grew up together. It's a small world, and many characters will cross over and pay a visit or two in several books. But, again, each novel stands on its own, and spoilers will be avoided as much as possible.

Dirty is a new series within the Camassia universe, and just like the other books taking place there, the Dirty Novellas stand on their own. They're a little shorter, quick fixes, with a bit more focus on the dirty filth. If you're interested in keeping up with the characters, the town, the timeline, and future novels, check out Camassia Cove's own page at www.ca-radeewrites.com.

One

Andrew Hart

"I thought I was going to have to send out a search party." I stepped out onto the rooftop terrace and walked over to where my little brother was sitting by the pool. The light from under the water was the only thing that illuminated the area; that, and his phone. "What did the doctor say today?"

I sat down on the lounger next to his and loosened my tie.

He pocketed his phone and knocked on his solid knee. "Cast's coming off tomorrow."

That was good news. Jace had been staying with me for the past three months after a grisly snowboarding accident up in Alaska, and I enjoyed having him here. He was too reckless for his own good, and I was a worrier.

"Glad to hear it." I cocked my head. "Is that why you're sitting up here moping?"

He should be ecstatic.

We worked together, and our positions at our company pretty much explained who we were as people too. He was the thrill-seeking nature photographer who jumped from mountain to mountain to discover hidden trails and wildlife. I was the sensible suit who ran the office and managed his talent.

In my spare time, I invested and dabbled in the stock market. He went skydiving. Come tomorrow, he could ease his way back into all that, and I would return to fretting.

Being the older brother—by eleven years, to boot—was a horrendous task.

Jace scrubbed a hand over his scruffy jaw and blew out a breath. "I think I wanna slow down a bit."

"You mean at work?" This was a surprise.

He nodded once. "Yeah. So, you know I made reservations at Coho for my birthday next week."

"Yes?" I furrowed my brow. Surely, our local steakhouse wasn't causing his broody behavior. We ate there more often than I cared to admit, and we'd gotten to know the owners well enough to call them friends.

"No one's coming." Jace raised his brows at me before they dipped in another frown, and he scooted back to recline in the lounge chair. "It's been like this for a few years now. I travel too much to keep buddies here at home." He lifted a shoulder and ran a hand through his hair. "I guess I miss it—having a social life. Being at home more."

Well, no one would be happier than me if he chose to work less or take on more local gigs. With one exception, my brother was the only family I had.

I'd discovered recently that spending time with friends didn't hold the same appeal anymore. That was why I was looking forward to this summer so much. Jace would—hopefully —be here, and my stepdaughter was coming home from college. Why Belle had insisted on studying overseas was beyond me.

"So I'll book fewer clients for you, then," I told him. "*National* wants you in Yellowknife in October, but—"

"I'll do that one," he said quickly, and I stifled a smirk. Underneath his rough I-don't-give-a-fuck exterior, there was a young man whose excitement for the wilderness bordered on boyish. He might be turning thirty, but to me, he was still seventeen in some ways. "It's only a month, right?" In response, I inclined my head. He nodded as well. "That's all right. Canada's closer. Just...less Asia and South America."

"Consider it done."

"Is this okay, though?" Some of his worry returned. "I don't know how shit's going, and this place ain't free." He waved a hand at the terrace.

I chuckled. It sometimes amazed me how oblivious he was. Not only did magazines and various other clients pay him handsomely, but I'd stopped taking pay for managing him once I'd built up my stock portfolio. While Jace and several other of my friends saw boredom in what I did, I saw the unpredictability, the ever-changing numbers, and the gamble.

"We're more than fine, little brother," I assured him. "I'm sorry you're stuck with only Belle and me for your birthday dinner, though."

His gaze snapped up. "Shit, I forgot she's coming home. When's that?"

"Has anyone ever said you live in your head?" I smiled wryly.

He laughed under his breath. "Maybe."

Maybe I told him that constantly.

"She's landing in Seattle in..." I checked my watch. "Approximately thirty-six hours."

I hadn't seen her in a year, and Skype was far from enough. She was busy and enjoying her life in London, which meant I was lucky if I got half an hour with her at the end of the week.

"Cool. Are we gonna do the multi-celebration this summer, too?"

"Of course," I replied. Given how rarely we saw one another these days, we planned for three days during the summer where we celebrated Thanksgiving, Christmas, and her birthday. Although, next January, I was planning on taking time off to go see her, so I would hopefully get to spend her twenty-first birthday with her in London. "I talked to her last Sunday, and her request was 'all the American food.'"

Jace laughed. "I know that feeling." Then he quieted and sighed contentedly. "It'll be good seeing her. I miss the little shit."

I almost snorted. Because the truth was, Belle was no longer Jace's *little shit*, as he so eloquently put it. In her two years halfway across the world, Belle had matured. She wasn't the lost little girl who mourned the death of her mother and didn't know what to do with her life. She was a stunning young woman who studied marketing and whose dimpled smile could light up a screen.

I made a dismayed face in the rearview mirror and rolled up the sleeves of my button-down. If my hair had been lighter, those spots of silver would have been less visible. Alas...they shone like a beacon.

Should I dye it?

"Are you becoming vain?" Jace asked.

"No, but evidently I'm becoming old," I muttered and left the car. Something was missing—and had been missing for a while. I couldn't put my finger on it, only that I wasn't content with my life anymore. As soon as I figured out what to change, I would. Until then, it looked like I'd be complaining about a whole lot. "You know, it wouldn't kill you to shave."

Belle coming home was a special occasion to me. Jace didn't have to look like a slob.

I'd made sure the cleaning service had been extra-thorough yesterday, and I'd ordered Belle's favorite flowers for her room. Or was I taking things too far? Was I too old-fashioned? I was going to spend the summer with my carefree little brother and my twenty-year-old stepdaughter; I wanted them to find me fun, too. I wasn't only the...parent, for lack of a better word.

Jace ignored my remark with a smirk, and we entered the bustling airport to bring Belle home.

"How the fuck are we supposed to find her?" Jace grunted, supporting himself on the crutch he'd had less than twenty-four hours and already hated with everything he was. "Christ, I hate people."

This from the young man who missed having a social life.

I couldn't blame him, though. Once upon a time, I'd loved Seattle. Now I was much more comfortable in our little town a couple hours north of here. An hour and a half, if Jace was behind the wheel.

As for Jace's question, I had an answer. "She's dyed her hair pink, she told me." I hadn't seen it yet myself because the last time we spoke, it was over the phone. I'd had this image of a shock of bright hair until her soft laughter had filtered through the receiver and she'd told me it was "faded magenta." Whatever that meant.

We stood in a sea of arrivals and their families, and I checked my watch. It'd been a while since she'd landed, so she should be here soon.

Jace made a noise. "Holy fuck."

"What, how pink is it?" I lifted my gaze, scanning the crowd.

"No, that's not... Uh."

I frowned at him, then searched for Belle some more, and—goddamn it all. Mother*fucker*. She emerged with a bright smile as she looked for us. I could only stare. My chest seized, and a flush spread up my chest. Unlike my brother, I'd known that she'd matured to an extent, and it was *still* a shock. Her gorgeous face had filled the screen of my laptop or phone whenever we Skyped; seeing her body was a whole other experience. And what the hell was she wearing? Those couldn't be called shorts. The denim rode up high enough to reveal her pockets. Underneath an open flannel shirt, a skimpy top hugged her generous curves.

"Keep that reaction to yourself," I told Jace, half irritated. With him or myself, I wasn't sure. Perhaps both. "Belle!" I started walking toward her so I could help with her luggage. Her hair was oddly cute, the long waves shifting in subtle shades of pink. My mouth stretched into a wide smile as she spotted me, and I even had to swallow a lump of emotion. At that point, I successfully pushed aside the unspeakable reaction I'd had, and I hurried to get her in my arms.

"Daddy-o!" She threw her arms around my neck, and I lifted her off the ground.

"God, I've missed you." Tightening my hold on her, I breathed in her light, sweet scent and reveled in having her home again. "My darling, why do you insist on living so far away?"

She laughed tearfully. "If it makes you feel any better, I can't wait to be done with uni."

That did make me feel better.

"Look at you, picking up local slang." Jace walked up behind us with a grin, and Belle was quick to give him a hug too. "When the fuck did you grow up?"

I shot him a look.

Belle smirked and wiped her eyes carefully. These days, she wore makeup. "My roommate taught me a lot. She's studying to become a stylist."

"There's not a thing you need to learn," I told her firmly and grabbed her roll-aboard. "You're beautiful as you are." Maybe a bit too beautiful.

"Such a dad response." She hugged my arm and held on as we made our way outside. "Can we eat at Coho? I'm *starving*."

"Anything you want, sweetheart." I kissed the top of her head.

Two

I woke up the next morning in a wonderful mood. Maybe this was what had been missing. For years, I'd had this three-bedroom loft all to myself. Now the rooms were full. Belle was home, and Jace occupied the guest room.

What're my chances of making him stay longer?

He had a cabin in Westslope, the northern part of town that was reserved for hermits who preferred to live in the middle of nowhere. His nearest neighbor was ten minutes of dense forest away. I was sure that was how he liked it, but he didn't have to get rid of the place. He could go up there whenever he wanted and still live here.

Or perhaps that was wishful thinking because I was becoming one lonely bastard.

After my shower, I yanked on a pair of sweat pants and a T-shirt. I didn't know what we were doing today, so this was the safe choice for a comfortable breakfast. I didn't even shave or put in my contacts. Glasses would do for now. Leaving my bedroom, I passed Belle's room, then Jace's before I got to the open space that made up the rest of my place. The kitchen, hallway, and living room blended together in brick and warm colors that'd started to feel cold to me.

This place was going to become a home again, a thought that hit me strangely. Because I hadn't noticed how dark it'd become until lately. Now, though... The pictures on the walls came to life in a new way when the two who appeared in most of the photos were under my roof.

I switched on the radio on the kitchen bar, then turned to pull out everything I needed from the fridge. Jace wanted eggs in the morning—a lot of them—and Belle woke up with a sweet tooth. She'd get pancakes today. My skills at making her favorite blueberry muffins were awful, no matter how religiously I stuck to the recipe.

The eggs were almost finished when Jace limped into the kitchen with a bed head and sleepy scowl.

"Morning, sunshine." I plated the scrambled eggs and added some sliced tomatoes and bacon bits. "Sleep well?"

"Sort of?" He squinted at nothing and scratched his head. "Um, are we gonna talk about last night?"

I furrowed my brow and slid the plate across the bar. "Did something happen?"

"You were *there*, Andrew. At Coho." He tucked into his food as if it was going to disappear, and I poured myself some cereal. "Something's changed with Belle. Jesus." He seemed baffled by something, though it was difficult to tell with the way he was hamstering the food in his cheeks. "Wasn't she crazy affectionate at dinner?"

"Hm." To be honest, I'd noticed it. "I wouldn't read into that." Certainly not when Jace was a pervert who'd just discovered his *niece*—his *niece*, for the love of God—was a very gorgeous young woman. "She missed us, Jace. She was excited to catch up."

And what a great evening it'd been. Over the best burgers and beers the town had to offer, Jace and I had mostly listened while Belle told us everything about her university and London. Some of the things, I already knew from talking to her. Her contact with Jace stayed at texting and occasional phone calls, so almost everything was new to him. Perhaps that was why the change appeared so drastic.

This had been a two-year-long process. From the two weeks I'd spent with her in London to help her get settled in before her freshman year...to now. Although, I could admit the biggest changes had happened this year, particularly the physical aspects.

I'd suppressed certain urges most of my adult life, making it second nature these days. I refused to dwell on the inappropriate. Besides, with everything Belle had going on, there were plenty of distractions. Ones that wouldn't send me to hell.

What I admired most about her was her passion. She was a spitfire and an activist, and animals and children were what she used her voice for to protect. She'd gotten so heated when telling us about a protest she'd been part of outside Parliament.

"Don't forget your place," I told Jace. "You're her uncle. She's not one of the girls you let hang around for a month before you trade her in for another."

He shook his head and forked up some eggs. "There's so much wrong with that sentence. First of all, we're not related. Second of all, I haven't gotten laid in almost a year, so don't paint me as some manwhore. Third of all—" he pointed the fork at me "—you're the one she was plastered to all evening, not me."

At that, I had to roll my eyes. "I'm the only parent she has.

Don't cheapen her affection because you suddenly have a hard-on for the wrong person."

If he pushed it, I might snap. Yesterday had been wonderful. Most of all, it was easy to keep her close when she seemed to want it that way. I'd had my arm around her throughout the evening, not because I possibly was a pervert too, but because I'd missed her very much.

"I won't," he replied. "But damn, I think I do. She's..." He shook his head. "Christ, she's sinful. And her wit...? She's always been able to make me laugh, but this was some next-level shit."

I wasn't fond of this topic. Jace had no shame, his honesty about this tumbling out too easily. It wasn't okay for him to be attracted to Belle. She'd been only eleven when I met her mother, and for the first birthday we'd spent as a new family, Jace had given her a jet-set Barbie that had a camera around her neck. She called Jace her uncle.

"Can I trust you to keep this to yourself?" I asked. "I won't stand for her becoming uncomfortable in her own home because you noticed she's developed curves."

"And those curves," he groaned. "Did you *see*—"

"Jace," I snapped.

"Oh, fine." He grumbled to himself and went back to inhaling his food.

Must be nice to be him in this position. Unlike me, he hadn't provided for Belle since she was a young child. She'd never called him Dad. Jace had come over for Sunday dinners and brought souvenirs to her from his adventures. Then he'd made his way to his home. His responsibilities had ended there.

I'd gone on to marry Belle's mother. I'd given Belle my name. And since her mother died of cancer six years ago, I'd been Belle's sole provider. Because who else was going to do it? They didn't know who her biological father was, and her mother's sister didn't show enough interest. We'd lost touch in recent years.

Damn if I was going to put Belle's well-being into the hands of people who treated her as an afterthought. No, I was her father, and I could continue to suppress my ridiculous urges. They probably weren't even urges, merely misplaced thoughts.

It had been a long time since I'd dated. Maybe it was time for me to get back out there. I certainly didn't mourn Belle's mother anymore, and I'd been a stepfather longer than I'd been a husband.

After this summer, I decided. I could join one of those dating sites, which held zero appeal. But it was time.

Shortly after, bare feet padded along the floorboards, and Belle appeared in the doorway wearing an old band tee of Jace's and a pair of cotton shorts. What was it with the length of shorts these days? Was fabric scarce?

Jace coughed into his coffee.

I hoped he burned himself.

"Good morning, darling." I rose from my stool and switched on the stove again. The pancake batter was waiting for me. "Take a seat and I'll make pancakes."

She grinned sleepily and walked over to me. "I'm so glad to be home." Sneaking under my arm, she wrapped her arms around my middle, and I chuckled. It truly was an affectionate girl who'd stepped off that plane. "Is there anything I can do, Daddy?"

I tilted my head.

Jace snorted behind us.

Daddy...

"No," I responded slowly as my mind started spinning. "You can relax and let me take care of this."

"'Kay." With a slight blush covering her cheeks, Belle pulled her hair into a high, messy bun at the top of her head, and then she left the kitchen area to turn on the TV.

"Is she for real?" Jace whispered. "She's never called you Daddy before, has she? The way she did it... Man, that's pure filth."

"Let it go," I whispered back, irritated. *Wound up.* There was nothing to read into here. I was a good father, damn it. Was it so incomprehensible that she'd missed me and was comfortable enough to let go of her adult thinking for a while? I was only glad. Children grew up too quickly, especially if they lost a parent too soon. Let her be my little sprite while she got rid of her jet lag and made herself at home again.

Come to think of it, she'd acted similarly the first week last summer. We'd barely left the loft, opting to stay in and watch movies and catch up. I could think of nothing I wanted more.

In fact, while I made the pancakes, I pulled out a notepad and jotted down a list of things to get at the market. It was going to be a week of favorites and indulgences, anything to coax out her beautiful smile and let her green eyes light up.

The sectional in the living room became our home for the following two days. Belle, after getting caught up on Jace's recovery, wanted to do some belated fussing to make sure he was okay. He sure as hell didn't complain. Sprawled out in the corner of the large sofa, he grinned like a king and greedily took every bit of attention.

"You'll stay here for the summer, though, right?" Belle plopped down next to Jace after rubbing his calf. "You shouldn't be alone up in the cabin."

"Listen to her, Jace." I took a sip of my coffee and changed the channel on the flat screen. "Belle, the movie you wanted to see starts now."

Jace grabbed the bowl of popcorn. "Hey, I'll stay until you kick me out."

That wouldn't happen.

Belle crawled over to me and decided to use my lap as a pillow.

I smiled down at her and combed back some stray hair from her forehead. The pink was growing on me, and it made her look even more carefree and youthful.

My movie picks were voted down quickly, so I read while Belle and Jace enjoyed action and horror. At one point, I tried to get up and leave so I could read in my room, but Belle didn't like that.

"It's not a family reunion if you're not here." The *duh* in her voice wasn't lost on me.

So I stayed and got lost in the latest book by Aiden Roe.

I emailed briefly with Jace's agent too.

Halfway through a second movie, he had a coughing fit.

"Are you all right?" I frowned.

He nodded and sat up straight, a closed fist covering his mouth. "Yeah—shit. A word?"

Belle sat too, so I could get up from the couch, and I told her I'd start dinner while I was at it. She and Jace had requested lasagna today.

"Okay, but tomorrow, I'm making dinner," she said. "You've done all the work."

Doting on her was hardly work.

Jace followed me to the kitchen, and he kept his voice down as I took out ingredients from the fridge.

"She's fucking indecent, Andrew." He started ranting under his breath. "Did you see her? She pulled her knee up—"

"Oh, that's crossing the line," I mocked. "I can't believe she lay down between us and put her *knee* up. The audacity."

He shot me an impatient look. "Are you finished?"

"Are you?" Because I was done hearing his accusations. Yesterday, he was sure she was taunting us by wearing another one of his T-shirts and a pair of my loose boxer shorts. To be fair, a lot of women wore those as pajamas. She was back in her own cotton shorts today.

"She's not wearing any goddamn panties, okay?" he snapped.

That halted me, and I glanced over at the couch to make sure Belle couldn't hear us.

Jace took a breath. "One leg down, one knee up. What the fuck do you think happens? I could see right up her—"

"That's enough," I replied hurriedly. "Just..." I didn't know what to say. Surely, she hadn't done...*that*...on purpose. To show him anything. It made me uncomfortable to consider. Even more uncomfortable was the image of her in my mind—sweet and unspoiled, and then...with her legs spread.

I cleared my throat and busied myself with preparing the ground beef.

Food—I was going to think solely of food. Making dinner, chopping vegetables, maybe even preparing snacks for tomorrow, or perhaps lunch. Suppress, suppress, suppress. Fantasies I'd had over the years, how drawn I secretly was to certain fetishes, were pushed down and locked into a box.

"I'll leave it alone." He lifted his brows. "But if it turns out I'm right... If she makes a move, I won't turn her down."

The anger that surged up within me took me aback, and I glared at his retreating form. Refocusing on the food, I heard him get comfortable on the couch with Belle, and her giggle made my blood boil. Was he serious? Was I the only one who saw how inappropriate this was?

Three

"**B**elle, dinner's..." *ready*. Fuck. The sentence died on my tongue as I stepped out onto the terrace upstairs. It was only a three-story building; would the fall kill me if I jumped? Because I was sure I deserved it.

These past few days, Jace's words had gone on a loop in my head, and I'd grown more...observant, I supposed was a good word. Everything Belle did, I analyzed. Was she being deliberately provocative? As she emerged from the pool in a skimpy bikini that didn't hide her delectable body whatsoever, I had my doubts.

Then again, kids nowadays wore too little in general. Right?

"Hi, Daddy!" She smiled widely and grabbed a towel from a lounger. "Is dinner ready yet?"

I nodded with a dip of my chin, staying by the door. I was having a difficult time looking away from her curvy little body. My skin felt hotter, and I cursed myself straight to hell. Her breasts were more than a handful. God, but she was lovely.

Sinfully so. When she turned around to get her phone, her perfect ass had my attention. Soft-looking, round, not even a little contained in her scrap of a bikini bottom. It jiggled as she fetched her clothes from another lounger, and then she was walking toward me again.

Northern Washington didn't get any tropical heat in the summer, and it showed. She shivered, and her nipples were tight little buds behind the white fabric.

A blazing trail of desire dropped to my gut. I had to let her walk ahead of me so I could adjust my erection.

I'm going to hell.

The shame was nearly crippling.

On our way down the stairs to the loft, Belle told me she was heading out next weekend to go dancing with some friends. In the meantime, I released a breath of relief when she finally pulled the large towel around her.

Then I replayed what she'd said and shook my head to clear it. "Where exactly are you guys going?" I asked. Because even though we'd begun our annual tradition of celebrating holidays in advance—starting with her birthday the day before yesterday—she wasn't actually twenty-one yet.

"I think this is one of those times where the less you know, the better," she teased.

I wasn't amused.

I trusted her, though. She'd never been too disrespectful—even in her hormonal, rebellious phase at seventeen—nor had she stumbled home drunk or broken any curfew.

"Hourly check-ins," I told her as we reached the door to the loft. "A text is fine, and you'll be home before two."

"Are you giving me a curfew?" She looked up at me with a scrunch of her nose.

I tapped it with a finger. "You bet I am." Opening the door, I headed to the kitchen and asked Belle if she could tell Jace that dinner was ready. His studio and my office took up the first floor of the building, and he'd been down there most of the day. When he was frustrated, tinkering with his camera equipment calmed him down.

Maybe it worked with sexual frustration as well, I didn't know. I hoped the kid suffered. Damn him for putting these thoughts in my head. As if Belle actually wanted anything from Jace—or me, for that matter. The latter was laughable.

Jace went to the gym for rehab on his leg after dinner, and I had work to do. A couple of hours of rearranging Jace's fall schedule was enough to cool my head, and then I lost another two once the Tokyo stock exchange opened.

I had a bathroom in my office, and when my eyes felt too heavy, I went in there to remove my contacts and switch to glasses instead. Then I was back behind my desk and my two computer screens.

"Daddy?"

My head snapped up, and I spotted Belle in the doorway. *Mother of God.*

This wasn't okay. I eyed her nightwear, a new baby-doll outfit that ended right below her ass. *What're you up to, little girl?* She was barefoot, and she shifted her weight.

"Yeah, baby?" Why the *fuck* did I call her that? I hadn't done that in...ever, really. Perhaps once or twice when she was sick.

"When're you coming up?" she asked. "I got a text from Jace. He's staying at the cabin tonight."

Why would he do such a thing? I wanted him here, away from rivers and mountaintops, while he was still in recovery.

"I should probably call it a night," I decided.

After powering off my computers, I followed Belle out of the office, and I locked up before we took the stairs to the third floor.

"I wish we had an elevator," she mumbled.

I chuckled.

To my surprise, she grabbed my pinkie. She made no comment, and she didn't look at me. It was a small gesture, a sweet one, yet it had an extreme effect on me. It opened the floodgates, and I was assaulted by desires put into words. I wanted to hold her close and protect her. I wanted to force my way deep inside her. I wanted to make sure she was always happy. I wanted her to kneel before me and take me in her mouth. I tried and fucking tried; I couldn't suppress the thoughts any longer. They swirled around my head all the way up to the loft.

What would it be like to visit her room at night, gently spread her legs, slip a hand under her panties, and touch her clit? Hell, what would it be like to *taste* her?

My chest suddenly felt tight. The onslaught of guilt nearly bowled me over, but there was a sick negotiator in me who claimed it was okay as long as I didn't act on it. Except, it wasn't okay. Not by a long shot.

"When Jace comes back tomorrow, can we have a sleepover on the roof?" Belle asked. "Like we used to? I miss those."

That was when we'd lived in our old house and she was *twelve*. The situation was entirely different now.

Don't pretend you'll say no.

I nodded once and fished out my keys. "Okay."

As I unlocked the door to our home, the shame flowed like a strong current in my veins, though it lost force—if only a little—when Belle lit up with joy. I was a sucker for her happiness. She had me completely wrapped around her finger.

I could survive a sleepover. They were fun affairs with tents, s'mores, and music. Nothing sexual about it. Jace would bring his guitar or harmonica, Belle would fill a tent with pillows and mattresses, and I would bring the food. The only music I played was the piano—not the easiest instrument to haul up to the roof.

Sleepover. Okay, I could swing that. No problem.

"She wants a *what?*" Jace hissed.

I pressed my lips into a grim line and grabbed another tomato to slice.

Jace began pacing on the other side of the kitchen bar, limp included, and every now and then, he stopped short and narrowed his eyes at me. He said nothing, probably because I didn't want to hear it.

"Sleepover," he scoffed.

"Lower your voice, please. She's in her room." Lifting the cutting board, I slid the vegetables into a glass bowl. "It's bad enough that I have to hear your wild theories."

I *hoped* they were wild. I hoped they were unfounded.

A moment later, a door opened and closed. It was followed by the front door opening and closing too, much like it had been doing all day. Belle was taking the sleepover seriously, and she'd been running upstairs with various items since breakfast. We weren't going to pitch a tent, she'd informed me. Instead, we were going to use the sunbed we had next to the barbecue area. It was positioned against the wall—close to the door leading to the stairwell—and it had a canopy with several layers of mosquito netting.

Comparing it to a regular bed, it was close to a king-size, so the space didn't worry me. It was the fact that I'd rather not have Belle getting pneumonia. It got cold here at night, regardless of season, but she assured me it would be "amazing." She was preparing the sunbed with everything we could need, and that was all she was willing to divulge.

"Are you attracted to her?"

Jace's question took me aback, and I had to take a breath before I could function again. I cleared my throat and checked on the meat I was marinating. It'd been soaking in oils and spices all day, and I deemed it ready for the next step.

"No bullshit, Andrew." His voice was low, bordering on gentle and full of curiosity. "You're on edge every time I bring this up, and—"

"Is that so fucking weird?" I whispered angrily.

He merely sat down on a stool and dropped his elbows on the counter, gaze intent. He'd inherited our mother's dark blue eyes. I'd inherited our father's steely grays. In a match between our parents, Mom had won every time. She'd been a force to be reckoned with. Jace had certainly gotten his adventurer's soul from her.

I swallowed and released a breath, realizing I was strung tight. It was almost impossible to relax my muscles. Placing my hands carefully on the tabletop, I inhaled through my nose and felt the defeat coursing through me. Perhaps I could've lied to my brother, but I didn't want to. The notion exhausted me.

Then I offered a small dip of my chin—*yes, I'm attracted to Belle; yes, I know there's something wrong with me*—and I did my damnedest to distract myself with dinner preparations. Jace and I liked the same meat for our skewers, while Belle preferred chicken. Jace loved mushrooms and hated bell peppers, while Belle shrugged at mushrooms and adored bell peppers—if they were red or yellow. Not the green ones. Everyone liked onions, and they preferred Cajun spices whereas I went with Buffalo sauce.

"It's okay, big brother."

It *wasn't*.

I could get on board with the erotic art and pornography I'd seen online, the kinks, and the lifestyles. I could accept women seeking comfort in the arms of the lovers they called Daddy, but *this*... It turned my stomach with how much I desired—No. God-fucking-damn. No, back into the box.

"Remember Vegas?" he asked.

My gaze, more like a glare, met his infuriatingly amused expression, and I was no longer angry. I was downright furious. Where the fuck was he going with this? Of course I remembered. In a poor attempt to "get me back on the horse" a few years ago, Jace had dragged me with him to Las Vegas. I'd endured two lap dances, one blow job from a prostitute—after which I'd felt incredibly uncomfortable—and then... Christ, I could barely think it. What was supposed to be a lap dance in a private room had morphed into much more than that, and I hadn't been alone with the stripper. I'd called it quits, thank goodness, but I'd come damn close to...to *sharing* a woman with my own brother.

He'd stayed behind and gotten lucky. I'd returned to our hotel and ordered an STD screening, and I'd made him promise never to mention that weekend again.

Then, when did "What happens in Vegas stays in Vegas" ever hold an ounce of truth?

"I could wring your neck," I replied curtly.

He laughed.

Dinner on the roof was relaxing and wonderful for the most part. Belle was curled up in a chair, chatting excitedly about this and that, and Jace had put his inappropriate agenda on the backburner to tease and banter. They had a way of jumping from dynamic to dynamic; sometimes they were almost like siblings, and sometimes she came to him for advice and help.

I was content to sit back and listen. I sipped my wine and gazed out over the pool, enjoying the moment. For now, there were no worries, no guilt, no shame.

My only trouble was the damn bed. Belle had filled it with blankets and pillows, string lights hanging from the fabric-covered ceiling, and she'd pushed the terrace's only heater closer to where we'd be sleeping. I supposed it would suffice, but I was a headcase regardless.

I had to make a decision about the highly inappropriate ideas Jace had gotten into his head—and mine. I had a feeling I wouldn't be able to enjoy much of anything before I made up my mind, and...and it was simply so wrong. I shook my head to myself and willed the images to stay away. They rattled me too much, and I wasn't even a worrier anymore because of them. I was neurotic. It wasn't who I wanted to be.

You can't go there. You can't think of her that way.

No, I seriously couldn't. Unfortunately, there was little I could do about my thoughts. They crept in unbidden no matter what I did. What I could do, however, was to never encourage anything. She could do whatever she wanted. I was going to remain a gentleman, and damn it all to hell, I was going to continue being the best father I could be for her.

I blew out a breath, feeling a bit more settled. This was going to work.

After dinner and too many s'mores, we went downstairs quickly to change into more comfortable clothes. Sweats and a long-sleeved tee should keep me warm throughout the night.

I had no idea what was taking Belle so long, but I had filled the dishwasher, returned to the roof, and helped Jace bring the snack bowls and the games to the sunbed by the time she reappeared.

She was dressed appropriately for once. Pajama bottoms, a cozy-looking flannel pair, and one of my old tees from college.

"Did you take forever so we would do all the work?" Jace tugged on her ponytail as he limped past her with the last of the snacks.

"*No*." She scowled at him and smoothed down her hair. "I had to shave my legs. They were a little scratchy."

"Well, come on, you two. What game are we starting with?" I carried over a side table that we could put our drinks on. Then

I shifted the layers of mosquito netting to the side and let Belle jump onto the thick mattress. She wore the most adorable smile.

"Monopoly!" she declared.

Splendid. I was going to win that. I was a bit of a Monopoly shark.

Jace snuck onto the bed too, taking the other side so Belle would be in the middle. That left me in charge of the heater and the drinks. My brother had set the cooler on the floorboards, so I poured a glass of Sprite for Belle and grabbed a handful of ice cubes from the box. Jace got a beer, and I went for another glass of wine.

Belle set up the game in the middle of the bed, and I scooted farther down the mattress so we were spread out. Besides, she needed the space for her countless bowls of candy. She already had a bowl full of gummy worms in her lap, and she was munching away while sorting through the stacks of Monopoly money.

My chest tightened at the sight of her carefree spirit. Could I love her more?

It was going to be a great night with my two favorite people.

"Oh my God, no!" Belle palmed her cheeks in horror as she landed on one of my hotels. "I can't—not again!"

I laughed. "Pay up, darling."

"I won't have any money left!" She got adorably angry and started going through what was left of her little stack.

Jace nodded at me and sucked in a breath, a signal I was hitting the right spot. His leg started cramping up about half an hour ago, so I was massaging the pressure points on his calf.

The foot of the bed had become mine, and I was lying side-ways across it to access his leg, my Monopoly fortune, and my last glass of wine. I'd set it on the elevated footboard and had already spilled twice—only a few drops, thankfully.

"You should know better than to play Monopoly with him," Jace reminded Belle with a tired chuckle. "What did you expect would happen?"

"I thought you'd go down first," she grumbled under her breath. "Okay, here's all I have. You're a meanie, Dad."

I winked and accepted the money. She was left with one little bill, and the next time she ended up on my property—or Jace's—she'd be out.

The game continued, and Belle got lucky for a few rounds. She raked it in when Jace landed on three of her hotels, and I commented that I would look after the money once she surrendered her winnings to me. That prompted her to throw a few gummy worms at my chest.

"That's sweet of you to bring me candy." I bit into one. "Tasty."

She was positively seething.

"Okay, I'm out." Jace leaned back and placed a hand under his head. "It's funnier watching Andrew piss you off, small fry."

"Can I have your money?" She batted her lashes at him while I removed his hotels and houses from the board.

"Fuck no, I wanna see you crash and burn." Jace smirked and finished his beer.

The tightness around his eyes had lessened, meaning he was no longer in pain. That was good. It'd worried me when he'd said he wasn't going to take his medication today since he was drinking. I would've preferred if he didn't drink and took his pain relief when he needed it.

"Okay, it's just you and me, princess." I sat up and rubbed a kink out of my shoulder.

"You're both meanies." She pouted. "Screw it. Daddy wins, I come in second, and—"

"The fuck?" Jace spluttered a laugh. "You're broke, Belle."

"But you quit the game," she retorted.

That started a new bicker war between the two, and I stayed out of it. While I packed away the game, my thoughts strayed to her new name for me, and I wondered if it was okay that I loved it when she called me Daddy. It probably wasn't, was it? Christ, I really was a pervert. I'd told my brother not to cheapen her affection for me, and here I was, linking Daddy to a fetish I'd sought out online more than once rather than seeing it for what it was, a substitute for Dad.

"I forgot he snores sometimes," Belle whispered.

I cracked a smile and kept gazing up, the millions of stars visible through the netting that covered the canopy of the bed. "It always soothed me to hear him snore."

Belle made a noise. "Why?"

Because then I knew he was home. Safe and sound. I knew I wasn't alone. "You know I worry when he's in some remote corner of the world."

She hummed and shifted closer, ending up using my shoulder as a pillow. "I love you, Daddy. Don't ever forget that."

Heavens, she knew how to squeeze my heart. "I love you more, darling." Slipping my arm underneath her instead, I hugged her to me and kissed the top of her head. "Are you cold?"

"A little," she admitted.

"You should've told me," I chided. Then I sat up and pulled my shirt over my head. I was lying next to the heater, and I'd had almost a whole bottle of wine; if anything, I felt hot. "Here, put this on."

We fumbled a bit in the dark until she was drowning in my

long-sleeved tee. The crisp air felt good on my skin, and I lay back against the mattress with a sigh of contentment. As she snuggled closer again, I made sure the duvet was up to her chin.

"This is nice." She made another humming sound and slid a hand up my chest. "We should have a sleepover every night." The reaction as she brushed her fingers through my chest hair was anything but innocent, and I cursed the amount of wine I'd had. It made it so much easier to enjoy her when that was the last thing I should do.

Closing my eyes, I surrendered to the pleasure of it. For one moment, I allowed myself to pretend this was all right. I stayed motionless, therefore guiltless. I wouldn't encourage anything, I repeated to myself. This was her doing.

The sensations kept flooding me and began to slow dance with sleep. My family was home; they were right here with me, safe and sound. What more could I ask for? I twitched when her fingers got a little ticklish along my lower stomach. They'd found the trail of hair below my belly button instead.

Her sweet touches and soft humming turned me into a listless being. It was as if my body had succumbed to the deepest of sleeps, yet my mind stayed relatively alert. Only sluggish and languid.

Just...not too sluggish not to notice when her fingers dipped underneath the waistband of my sweat pants.

"Daddy?" she whispered. "Are you sleeping?"

Oh Christ, little girl, why are you asking me that?

She moved her hand to my hip, and I could hear how her breathing changed.

"Daddy," she whispered again.

I kept my mouth shut and my breaths even. I wasn't a good man, certainly not a gentleman. There was one reason and one reason only I didn't say anything, and it was to see what she'd do. I was hoping against hope she'd do something nefarious.

"*Daddy*," she said a little louder.

The only response was Jace's quiet snoring.

Belle seemed to relax further in my arms. Inch by inch, she shifted her hand around my hip, acting as if she didn't have an agenda. At this point, I could sense it. It wasn't a hope. I knew. Jace had been right all along.

A low rumble of thunder rolled in, and it took me a second to realize it was happening inside of me. Perhaps I was finally losing my mind. Because every time she moved, a part of me grew darker and more depraved.

She was doing this to me. My sweet, innocent little girl wasn't so innocent, after all.

I counted the seconds until the very tips of her fingers ghosted along my cock outside my sweat pants, and that was it. Everything was about to change. Come tomorrow, I couldn't promise I'd keep my word on just about anything I'd said in the past.

I swallowed and let out a slow breath, and Belle's fingers continued tracing the length of my cock. *You filthy fucking baby.* I couldn't believe her. She'd had me so duped. I'd *defended* her against my brother's accusations.

A white-hot rush of desire flooded me when she applied pressure and palmed me, or as much as she could. Her breathing sped up a bit again, possibly because I was growing hard. My jaw tensed, and I had to tell myself to un-fucking-clench.

What would it be like to flip her over right now and fuck her?

Images I'd cursed myself for swirled in my head. From the sweetest fantasies of kissing her hungrily while she rode my cock like a good girl...to the darkest urges that summoned me to claim her, to pin her down with force and fuck her until her little pussy was overflowing with my come.

Belle touched me curiously, her hand sliding down to cup my balls and trace the outline of them, then up again to caress and stroke. Once my cock was rock solid, she rubbed me from base to tip over and over. She seemed frustrated that my clothes were in the way, and frankly, so was I. But I wasn't going to let her go too far. Now that I knew she was nothing close to innocent, it was time to regain some control.

Fuck feeling guilty.

I maintained my composure for the better part of the following day. Mainly because Jace was with his physical therapist and then working in his studio, and I wanted to discuss everything with him before I did anything.

I *was* going to do something. Belle had made me snap last night, and since then, I couldn't find an ounce of remorse in me, nor could I find the strength to deny myself. She'd let out the cutest little whimper, bordering on a whine, when I'd eventually rolled over and refused her access to my cock, which had sparked the question. How far had she been planning to go? Far enough, that was for certain. No. No more pretending to be someone I was not. I didn't know how far I could take this, how far I *dared* to take it, but the box that'd been rattling quietly in the back of my mind had been opened.

I ached to push her. I wanted to push her *hard*. She'd had her fun, and it was my turn now.

I didn't know what I wanted to start with, punishing her for being devious or using her for my pent-up possessiveness and selfish hunger. The mere thought of forcing my way between her thighs and spreading her open for my cock made my heart accelerate. Oh God, could I really—

"Are you trying to chop through the cutting board?"

"Jesus." I sucked in a breath and took a step back at the sound of Jace's voice. Inspecting the damage, I supposed his question was valid. The peppers I'd been chopping were almost liquid at this point. "You're home." I took another calming breath and set down the knife. "We have to talk. I think I've gone insane."

His eyes brows went up. "Is everything okay?"

I shook my head, then peered around him to make sure Belle wasn't in the hallway or had the door to her room open. "Far from it. Let's sit down."

Jace wasn't particularly surprised to hear what I had to say about last night, aside from the part where she'd chosen a time when we were both in bed with her to, for lack of a better word, explore.

For the sake of my sanity, I had to ask him if I was sick to want her, and his response offered both relief and resignation.

"Fuck that, big brother. She's got the biggest heart and, evidently, the dirtiest mind. How's a guy to resist? Besides, even if it were sick, it seems we're all in the same boat."

I groaned internally and scrubbed my hands down my face. *Sick, sick, sick.* Yet, I knew the time for pretending was over. I'd watched her all day, and nothing could quench my thirst for her. She'd been on her stomach on the floor while watching cartoons this morning, ankles crossed in the air, and it'd been a miracle I hadn't taken her right then and there. Her giggles filled my cock with blood and arousal.

"I want to force myself on her," I admitted with the last shred of decency in me. "I don't want her to go back to London. I want her here—in my bed, spread out for me."

Jace cleared his throat and shifted on the couch. "Yeah, I,

uh, I can understand why those thoughts would make you feel guilty—"

"You think?" I snapped. Heavens, I was too strung tight to even hold a conversation.

"Easy," he replied mildly. "You gotta keep in mind that she's put those ideas there. She's not merely a woman in a short skirt. She's done this on purpose, and last night she literally touched you while you, for all she knew, were asleep. If you wanna talk about crossing lines, start with her." He had a point, and I clung to it. "My turn to tell you something." He paused and threw a glance over his shoulder, down the hall. "I went through her computer the other day, and the porn she's got on there... It's fucking rape fantasy central."

"Christ," I whispered. I rubbed a hand over my mouth, trying to picture my girl being into that filth. "*Christ.*"

"I gotta know something, Andrew." There was something off about Jace's voice that made me push Belle out of my mind for a minute. He looked less confident. "You have to be honest. Do you want me to go back to my cabin? I won't be offended, and with me outta the way—"

"No." The word left me without a moment of consideration, because the thought was akin to torture. For so long now, I'd wanted my family here with me, and *damn* if I was going to let him break us up. I'd been promised a summer, and I was going to take it. Then, the more I thought about what he was implying, my answer grew more resolute. "Jace, she's been indecent toward both of us." And there was no trace of jealousy. If anything, I wanted to use this. Anything to keep us together as a family—at least for the summer. And when Belle returned to the UK, I'd want him here more than ever. "You're staying, and that's final."

That earned me a rare glimpse of the boy he used to be. He

did always turn to me for advice and reassurance, and I had no plans on that ever stopping.

"Okay." He smiled and nodded once. "So, what happens now?"

I had a couple ideas that would send us in the direction I wanted to explore, immoral as it might be.

Five

"I'm gonna go get apples, Daddy."

I looked away from the jar of peach preserves I was inspecting and eyed her over the rims of my glasses. "We're already going to the produce, darling."

"I know, but I'm restless." She toed the floor and shrugged. "You can meet me there, okay?"

"Sure." I stifled my smile and returned my attention to the preserves. Jace wanted to test his leg strength by going on a one-day hike next weekend, and I wanted to make sure he brought his favorite sandwiches. With one jar of strawberry and one peach in the cart, I continued down the aisle. At the end of it, the produce section waited—along with Belle's restlessness, it seemed.

Good.

She was noticing the past couple of days' changes, and she didn't quite know what to do about it.

I'd stopped trying to fit in, for one. I no longer cared if she and Jace found me *fun* to be around. I was a man in my forties, and I wanted things done a certain way. I had my hobbies and interests; Belle and Jace had theirs. Mine came first now.

If Belle wanted to be my little girl, she'd abide by my rules too.

Jace had reacted oddly well to my adjustment. Usually so headstrong and cocky, he appeared almost eager to take the back seat. I knew comfort when I saw it, and I'd cursed myself for a day and a half for not having seen this sooner. It wasn't only the worrier in me he appreciated. Much like Belle, he required authority as well. Someone to ground him when he wasn't out on his adventures. A place of stability, and that was what our home was becoming.

After grabbing a jar of the peanut butter he preferred, I pushed the cart to the produce section, where I found Belle picking out strawberries. She held a plastic bag of green apples in her hand, and she put them in the cart after spotting me.

"I'm gonna make apple pie after dinner," she said with a grin.

Let me condition that statement just a bit.

"We're eating out tonight, I'm afraid. You'll have to make it another night." I took the carton of strawberries from her and grasped her chin gently, moving in closer. "I like it when you ask."

Her eyes widened before she quickly composed herself and swallowed audibly. "I'm sorry, Daddy," she whispered. "I'll ask next time."

"Good girl." I pressed a kiss to her nose, then placed the strawberries in the cart. "We need a zucchini."

She stumbled and flushed. "A z-zucchini?"

Filthy little princess whore.

"Yes, for dinner tomorrow."

Leaving my bedroom, I rolled up the sleeves of my button-down and aimed for the living room. Jace and Belle were still getting ready, so I could watch the news before we left for dinner.

"Dad!" Belle hollered. "Where are we going?"

"The steakhouse," I called back and folded one leg over the other. I let the remote rest on my thigh and watched a segment on some wildlife accident.

"But you told me to dress up." There was confusion in her voice now.

I smiled to myself. "I like seeing you in dresses, baby girl."

There was silence after that.

Jace was next to appear. Instead of taking a seat next to me, he chose to watch the news with me while pacing absently. He was consumed with rehabilitating his leg, and it was working. He took less of his medication, and his limp wasn't as noticeable.

"You seem more comfortable," I noted, pleased.

The corners of his mouth twisted up. "I was gonna say the same about you. No shaving, no contacts?"

I rubbed a hand over my jaw. Truth be told, shaving had always been one of those things I did automatically. Our father would have a fit if we didn't look professional. But lately, I'd realized I mostly did it to hide the gray in it. And I was done with that. I kept it trimmed, though there was no reason to obsess over it.

"I am." I inclined my head. Same applied for the glasses. They were much more comfortable than sticking my fingers in my eyeballs every morning.

"Good." Jace looked down the hall and raised his brows. "Damn, little girl."

It prompted me to look over my shoulder, and Jace wasn't wrong. *Damn.* Belle had donned a lovely wraparound dress, perfect for summer and perfectly matching her hair. Even the ballet flats she'd put on her dainty feet were adorable.

"Come here, darling." I held out a hand to her, loving that I no longer had to hide my reaction to her. "Show Daddy your dress."

She'd carried herself much more demurely this past couple of days, and it was with an unsure look in her eyes and rosy cheeks that she walked over and gave me a little twirl.

My eyes raked up her slender legs, the shapes of her exquisite curves, lingering over her ample cleavage, and settled on her beautiful face.

"I might be biased, but I think I have the most gorgeous daughter on the planet." I leaned forward and slid a hand up the inside of her smooth leg. *Fuck me.* How was I going to keep my hands off her? She was all cream and softness.

Belle averted her gaze and looked positively flustered, yet she took a step closer and wrung her hands awkwardly. "Do you really think so?"

"Definitely," I murmured, unable to tear my eyes away from her legs. I lifted the dress a few inches and brushed my fingers along the start of her thigh, and it took every bit of self-control not to go higher.

"I'm sure you're popular with all the boys, aren't you?" Jace rounded her and sat down on the armrest next to me.

Belle had no idea what to do with our attention. "Um, I-I guess. I haven't really—I mean, I don't find them very interesting."

"Why's that?" I glanced up at her, never removing my hand from her thigh. It gave me a dark thrill to see her so out of sorts.

She lifted a shoulder and sucked her bottom lip into her mouth.

"Use your words, girl," Jace told her.

She didn't, at first. She seemed rooted in place, frozen, as my hand slipped higher up. *So much for self-control.* I put the blame on her. She'd started this. She'd woken up two fuck-hungry beasts.

"Obey your uncle." I pinched the inside of her thigh, hard enough to cause her to jump. "Surely, there's been someone you've liked."

She gulped and turned her head. Anything to avoid eye contact. Had her cheeks ever been that pink? They were fucking stunning.

"No," she whispered.

Sweet Jesus. Was there a chance she was actually a virgin? It was incomprehensible.

"That's good, hon." Jace took a gentler approach and grabbed her hand, kissing the top of it. "There's only one thing those little shitheads want anyway."

How true. "I have half a mind to forbid you to date altogether." In fact, I should. I stroked her higher still, until I came into contact with soft, *wet* cotton.

Belle startled and finally looked at me, her eyes as wide as saucers. Her chest heaved with a stuttering breath.

I clenched my jaw, and my nostrils flared. The girl was wet, and it sent me spiraling. "You want to keep this safe from them." I gently scratched the surface of her panties with the tip of my finger. Tickling the spot right above her clit.

In my periphery, I caught Jace adjusting his cock.

If Belle's gaze dropped, she'd see the bulge in my own pants.

"Do I make myself clear, darling?" I asked and withdrew my hand. "You have better things to focus on than hormonal boys."

She jerked her head in a nod. "Okay."

"Good." I rose from my seat and dipped down to kiss her cheek. "Let's go eat. I'm famished."

We walked to the steakhouse, and Belle surprised me by holding my hand. It made me question where her sense of self-preservation was. Jace and I were the ones who caused her discomfort and uncertainty, and rather than putting distance between us, she clung.

It was a wonderful summer evening and a nice stroll down the cobblestone streets, the sun dipping behind the mountains and low buildings. We walked past seemingly normal families and couples, and I couldn't help but wonder what they saw when they passed us. Were we also a normal-looking family? Despite how young Belle was at twenty, she'd long since exceeded the age where a daughter held the hand of her father.

Pride and possessiveness built up inside me, and I grasped her hand tighter. She was an extraordinary girl in my eyes, and I was fine with however strangers viewed us. Father, daughter. Man with a younger lover. Family.

I wanted to believe she'd been brought into my life for more than one reason.

"Andrew, hold up." Jace had stopped on the sidewalk. I assumed his leg was hurting until I saw he'd spotted someone across the street. It was a man my brother's age and...hmm, his boyfriend, judging by how affectionate they were. "I'll be right back."

Belle and I waited outside a bookstore, but her usual exuberance for books was nowhere to be seen.

Concern hit me squarely in the chest. "Is everything okay, baby?"

She looked up from the ground and nodded quickly. "Yeah. Um. I was wondering, though..." She broke eye contact and bit her lip. "Have I done something wrong, Dad?"

"What makes you think that?" I tucked a piece of hair behind her ear.

She flushed and stammered. "I-I don't know. Things feel... um, d-different."

Oh, really... "Like what?" I stepped closer and lifted her chin. Her captivatingly green eyes called to me; it was the vulnerability in them. "Tell me, sweet girl." I stroked her cheek.

But she couldn't. I knew she couldn't put voice to the atmosphere that'd changed around the house or my behavior or how Jace had tucked her into bed last night. Because if she did, she'd leave herself exposed for my response. Would I call her silly for reading into things? Would I kiss her? Would I call her out for her inappropriate touching?

"It's probably nothing," she mumbled and looked down.

I smirked, then kissed her on the forehead. "You've done absolutely nothing wrong. You're my perfect little girl, aren't you?"

As she lifted her hands, I noticed her fingers were trembling. She fidgeted with a button on my shirt. "I want to be. I miss you tons and tons when I'm in London. Uncle Jace, too."

"Oh, my princess." I hugged her to me, loving her beyond words. I *craved* her. In old ways and new. I fucking hungered for her. "We miss you more." I used my hands more freely than I would've a few weeks ago. I stroked her back, her sides, brushing a thumb underneath her breast...and let one hand pat her bottom. "I adore having you home," I murmured into her ear and breathed her in. That sweet scent filled my lungs, clinging as much as she did to me.

She craved too. The only question was just how much she wanted.

She'd lost the choice there.

Jace and I were going to take it all. I could see no other outcome anymore.

Even now, holding her, comforting her, my cock grew hard,

demanding to stake a claim, and I didn't hide it for shit. If anything, I pressed it against her belly to make sure she felt it.

It shoved her further outside of her comfort zone.

I'd pay just about anything to read her mind. What could she be thinking? Was she wondering if I was unaware? Or how I could be pretending as if nothing was going on?

Jace was about to wrap up his conversation. I saw him in the bookstore's window. He grinned and shook hands with the taller of the men and bumped fists with the other.

I patted Belle's bottom a couple more times, lingering a bit too long, perhaps, and broke the hug. I deserved an award for letting go of that soft, round, perfect flesh.

"Who was that?" I asked Jace.

"Casey. A guy I went to college with," he replied with a smile. "Or, we took a few classes together. We're gonna meet up for beers sometime."

"That's nice." I was happy for him; he did need more local friends. Now that I was reestablishing myself in his life, I didn't have to envy the people he was with. Jace would make time for both friends and family.

I should follow his lead, in fact. I'd neglected my friends this summer. One night out wouldn't hurt. I could pick one of the few nights Belle was out with her own friends. For the most part, she chose to meet up friends during the day, only to return an hour or two later and claim she was bored.

Six

"I don't wanna walk," Belle whined.

"We're almost home," I chuckled.

She'd been plastered to Jace until his leg declared the extra passenger too much, and now she was leaning heavily on me for the last two blocks. Our little lightweight. Since we knew Adam and Alessia, the owners of the steakhouse, quite well, Alessia had winked and looked the other way when we'd ordered Belle a glass of champagne. We let her indulge sometimes, but perhaps three glasses had been too much. She clearly couldn't handle her alcohol.

"Can I piggyback you, Daddy?" She pouted up at me, eyes glazed.

I smiled and tapped her nose. "No, but tell you what. I'll carry you." Slipping my hands under her armpits, I hoisted her up and positioned her on my hip. "Wrap your legs around me. There we go—oh, your arms are cold, darling."

"I don't feel nothin'." Her singsong voice tickled my ear as she burrowed closer.

"Bubbly will do that to you, sweetie," Jace said.

I felt her smile against my neck.

I rubbed her bare arm to warm her up as best I could. Meanwhile, my other hand was firmly cupping her bottom underneath her dress. Belle acknowledged it by squirming once I slid my pinkie between her legs, resting it atop the tempting slit of her pussy. I couldn't help myself. She'd been teasing us all evening, intentionally or not. She was our little comedian, and she loved to make us laugh.

I wanted her panties wet again.

"You're not like other dads," she whispered for only me to hear.

I pressed a kiss to her forehead and let the rest of my hand join my pinkie. Why even bother acting like I wasn't minutes away from sinking my cock inside her? I'd waited long enough.

She gasped and froze for a beat, then slowly relaxed and shifted over my hand.

"I'm willing to bet you're not like other daughters either," I whispered back.

Her breathing hitched as I teased my index finger right into the soft crease between her thigh and pussy. It would be so easy to slip that digit underneath her panties.

"Do—do you like having me as your daughter?"

"No, I love it, baby. You're the best daughter a father could ask for."

"Oh," she breathed. "Okay, good."

———

She was asleep in my arms by the time we arrived home, and my thighs were on fire after I'd walked up three flights of stairs with her. I considered myself in shape for my age, but I was no athlete. Jace had to take over when we entered the hallway, and he carried her into her room.

I joined them shortly after and leaned against the doorframe while my brother put her to bed. It was, to be honest, one of the most beautiful sights. Belle's room was a shrine to the boy bands and dance classes of her teenage years, with an abundance of books and trinkets.

Everything on her bed was pink and yellow. Pillows, duvet, blankets, and even a few stuffed animals.

She pouted and mumbled, half asleep. He helped her off with the dress and murmured compliments to her.

"Do you know how gorgeous you are?" With the dress on the floor, he leaned over her to unhook her bra. Belle yawned a thank-you and rested her forehead on his hip, and her arms came up to hug his thigh.

"I love you, Uncle Jace."

"Love you too, sweetie." He removed her bra and helped her get under the covers. And the second her head hit the pillow, she was out with a sleepy smile.

Jace rubbed his fingers over her nipples until they pebbled, a scene I couldn't tear my eyes away from. It was the first time I'd seen her breasts. They were full yet perky, perfect to fuck. And I couldn't blame my brother for lowering his head to kiss them. He wrapped his lips around a nipple and sucked, only to do the same with the other a beat later.

I adjusted my erection.

"Sleep well, little niece." He finished with a kiss to her cheek, and he pulled the covers over her before leaving her side.

The lust was written all over him.

"When?" His whispered question left no confusion.

I switched off the light. "Tonight." We were done waiting. It was time to take her. "And bring your camera."

About an hour later, we'd showered off the evening and discussed how we were going to play this. We had the same goal, same wishes, and neither of us was very keen on hearing Belle's opinions tonight. She'd begun this. Now we ran the show. End of.

I still wore my towel around my hips, whereas Jace had put on a pair of boxer briefs that already looked uncomfortably tight. On the way to Belle's room, I handed my brother a bottle of numbing spray and a jar of coconut oil. I might need it myself, though our girl's ass was my main concern.

"I don't want her in too much pain."

He nodded and twisted the products in his free hand. The other held his camera and a small tripod.

There wasn't going to be any finesse with my taking of her. I'd lost my patience, and all I wanted was to be balls deep inside her. With impatience came discomfort, but the spray should ease some of it.

Sneaking in to her pitch-black room, I let the sliver of light from the hallway guide me to her bed. She slept peacefully on her side, and I felt the familiar stirrings of possessiveness and love in my chest. Fuck, but she was lovely. Perfection. And she would finally belong to me—us—in every sense of the word.

I carefully pushed aside the thick duvet and parted her knees, and she made a sleepy sound and rolled onto her back. With my breath caught in my throat, I hooked my fingers underneath her panties and slipped them off slowly. Waiting for me was the sexiest sight I'd ever witnessed. Her smooth, bare little pussy. Just watching her made my heart race, and blood continued to flood my cock.

I got comfortable between her thighs and eased my thumbs over the silky lips of her pussy. Jace was ready, and that was good enough for me. I leaned in and brushed my lips to her flesh. Her sweet scent invaded my senses as I breathed her in and slowly teased her slit with the tip of my tongue.

A groan rumbled in my chest the instant her flavor hit my taste buds. Knowing I'd only have a few seconds of eating her out before she woke up to the touches, I succumbed to my thirst. I spread her pretty little lips with my fingers and tongued her greedily. My mouth closed over her clit, and I sucked on it until she stirred and mumbled her complaint. It wouldn't be a complaint for very long.

"Shh, Belle." Jace stroked her cheek while he rubbed his cock through his underwear.

His camera was set up on the nightstand.

"She's waking up." I swirled my tongue across her lips, farther down, and circled her tight opening. I didn't want to prepare her too much, but I had to feel her. I wriggled the tips of two fingers inside of her, and my cock throbbed. "I'm gonna need lube, little brother." Wetness had started building up, though the few drops I licked up were far from enough.

I tore off the towel, and Jace got the numbing spray and coconut oil.

By now, my eyes had adjusted to the darkness.

"Do I tiptoe around modesty, or...?" He quirked a brow.

I smirked faintly and lowered my face to fuck Belle's hole with my tongue, and it was enough of a response for him. My hands were occupied. His weren't.

He scooped up a generous amount of the thick, buttery oil and greased my cock. The lubricant melted under his fingers, and I groaned at the indulgence. At the same time, Belle shook off the remnants of sleep that clung to her, meaning we were out of time.

"Wh...*ungh*... What..." She rubbed her fists against her eyes.

Quickly grabbing the bottle, I spread her pussy lips and gave her opening two sprays. It would be enough, I hoped. Then I crawled up her delectable body as Jace wiped his hand and picked up the camera.

"I'm sorry, but Daddy can't wait."

My cock jutted out, thick and glistening, and I gave it two quick strokes and dragged the head between her pussy lips. It was then that Belle gained awareness and widened her eyes in shock. And that look—that one, right there—did me in. The innocence, the exposure, the disbelief. With a low growl, I pushed my cock at her and shoved it deep inside of her.

The pleasure was blinding and robbed me of my breath. A scream pierced the fog I suddenly found myself in, but my only answer was to slap a hand over her mouth.

"We're done with your games," I bit out through clenched teeth. Mother of God, the sensations were indescribable. They rippled down my spine, zinged and zapped between pleasure points, and swallowed me whole.

Peering down between us, I withdrew my cock, only to push again. Belle cried out once more, her body stiff as a stick.

"You feel incredible, darling." I started fucking her at a slow pace, wanting her to feel every inch that stretched her to the max. "You have the tightest little baby cunt, don't you?" I dragged my gaze back to her beautiful face and kissed her cheek. Even her tears were delicious. "Is Daddy your first?" I whispered. "Tell me. Tell me if Daddy's cock is the first to fuck your pretty pussy."

Something other than pain swam in her big eyes. It wasn't terror or fear.

The tightness around her eyes faded too. A low, muffled sob escaped her, and she closed those gorgeous peepers, causing another two tears to fall down her cheeks. But a hoarse moan followed, and her body was relaxing. Accepting me.

"I've wanted this for so long," she whimpered from behind my palm.

"Oh, my baby, why didn't you tell us?" It was safe to remove my hand and put it to better use. I got my hands on her breasts at long last, and I cupped the soft flesh and stared as her nipples constricted.

"I didn't know how," she whined. "Ow, Daddy—ow, ow."

"So you thought it would be better to touch your father in his sleep?" I plucked at a nipple and pinched it. Mortification was etched across her features, and she tried to hide her face from me. "You think I wouldn't notice if my own daughter touched my cock?"

"I couldn't help myself."

That seemed to be the weak defense of all of us.

"I wanted to know what it would feel like," she croaked.

I grunted and pushed in harder. "Now you know." Grabbing her jaw, I finally got to kiss her. Like the rest of her, her lips were soft and pliable and addictive. I twisted my tongue around hers and kissed her until she pushed at my shoulders. Only then did I let her turn away and gasp for air. "Your uncle and I are going to fuck every little hole in your body, Belle. We'll make sure you know they belong to us. We won't be done until they're dripping with come."

She let out a wail, and her cunt constricted around my cock.

"We'll never be done," Jace murmured.

He was right.

"Oh God, oh God, oh God..." Belle chanted breathlessly and dug her fingernails into my biceps. If she was still in pain, the pleasure overrode it.

"Back away so I can film her pussy," Jace whispered.

I took another intoxicating kiss, then eased back on my haunches. With two fistfuls of her ass, I pulled her along so I wouldn't slip out of her completely. Jace gave us a warning that

pushed some hair away from her face. "We just want to show you how much we want you."

She shuddered violently and burrowed into my embrace. It was the hand-holding all over again. She crawled toward the predator and hoped for sanctuary. Reckless little girl. She was lucky we were here.

"We'll take care of you." I peppered her face with kisses as Jace lubed his cock. "Here, baby." I twisted my body and reached for the nearest stuffed animal. "Your bunny can comfort you while we turn you into our little fuck doll."

She hugged the bunny tightly, making me impossibly ravenous for her.

Jace was ready, so I picked up Belle carefully, staying inside of her, and changed our position. It would be easier for him to take her if I was on my back and had Belle's ass in the air.

Belle stayed snuggled against my chest with her stuffie. "Is it gonna happen now, Daddy?"

"Yes, it is. Can you give me some sweet kisses?"

She lifted her head and pouted at me.

"Do you want us to stop?" I lifted a brow.

She shook her head quickly and kissed me. *Thought so.* I slid my hands down her body and palmed her bottom, spreading her cheeks for her uncle. At the same time, I thrust up into her and earned myself a few delightful gasps from her.

"Why does this feel so right?" she whispered shyly, breathless.

I smiled, love swelling up within. "It does feel right, doesn't it?"

She nodded and sucked her bottom lip into her mouth. "I've thought about you and Uncle Jace since before uni."

"Dirty girl." I released her lip from her teeth. "Did you save yourself for us too?"

Another nod. "But it was only a fantasy. I didn't think anything would happen—not really."

I hummed and waited to respond. Jace got settled between my legs, and the moment Belle tensed up, I knew he was touching her. Preparing her.

"Kiss him." I grasped her shoulders and lifted her off my chest. "I want to see my two favorite people love each other."

It looked so damn right. Jace locked an arm underneath her breasts, and she tilted her head back. It was a passionate kiss they fell into, as if they'd done this a million times before. Their tongues danced sensually. She twisted her fingers in his hair, and he stroked her tits. And whenever she whimpered in pain or stiffened from his fingers in her bottom, he paid extra attention to make her relax again.

The bunny stayed in Belle's grip.

My breathing sped up as Jace stretched her, because it was my cock that reaped the rewards of her body's struggles. Every time she tensed, every time she squirmed.

I stroked her thighs and hips, inching closer to her pussy with every pass. Being so much larger than her had some advantages. She was slight enough for me that when my fingers brushed over her hip bones, I could almost reach her pussy with my thumbs. Those were the ghosting touches that seemed to conflict with her discomfort. One second, as Jace stretched her asshole, she whined and tried to move away. The next, as my thumbs tickled the sensitive skin at the junction of her thighs, she moaned and rolled her hips over my cock.

"You want more, darling?" I asked.

"*Yes*," she pleaded. "You're just teasing me, Dad."

Well, I supposed it was best to stop teasing her, then.

I nodded at Jace.

"Come here." I coaxed Belle to my chest again and trapped

my hand between us. "If you're a good girl for Jace and take his cock, I'll make you come. How's that?"

"Probably impossible," she mumbled.

I chuckled. Perhaps being nice to her didn't work, because she had a vastly different reaction when I used her roughly. That was okay. I could be a bastard without a problem.

Belle gasped and went rigid when Jace started pushing inside her. His features were drawn tight from restraining himself.

"This is gonna go one way or the other," I whispered against Belle's hair. "Either you relax and let Jace fuck your ass, or he takes you until he tears you up. Are we clear?"

She shook and exhaled around a whimper. "I'm trying."

I wriggled my hand farther south and stroked her pussy. "Try harder." To give her a taste of what was to come if she behaved, I scissored her clit between my fingers and rubbed her firmly. The slow, hard circles seemed to do the trick. "Is this how you touch yourself at night? Like this?"

She couldn't speak, only nod. My brother was gritting his teeth, hands gripping her hips, and forcing his cock deeper, and it was taking the ability to speak away from her. Her breaths grew choppy and shallow.

I felt how Jace claimed her. She had my cock in a wet vise, and it got tighter for every inch he pushed in.

"Oh, fuck..." He leaned forward and dropped his forehead to Belle's back. For a moment, all I heard was their labored breathing.

"It h-hurts," Belle panted.

"It's supposed to." I couldn't wait any longer. I shifted my hips, then slid deeper, through her sweet juices. "You asked for this. You could've told me I had a filthy fucking daughter, but no, you had to be a sneak."

Jace set the pace, fucking her in long, unhurried strokes, and

I mirrored him. When he pulled out, I pushed in. It kept her desperate little cries and moans constant.

We fucked with her head, praising her one second, and calling her out on her immoral behavior the next. We did the same with pleasure and pain. My brother took over and played with her clit while I stroked and manipulated her breasts.

"Goddamn, she feels good," Jace groaned.

"Fuck her harder," I growled.

I hadn't been bullshitting when I'd said I wanted to push her. More than that, I was starting to believe it was what she got off on. Because the faster we took her, the longer her moans became.

"You like this, don't you?" I clenched my jaw. My fingers dug into her flesh hard enough that she'd have bruises tomorrow. "Have I raised a pain whore, Belle?"

"Oh my God," she wailed. Sweat-dampened hair stuck to her face, and I swore she'd never been more gorgeous. Unfiltered, dirtied-up, flushed, mascara smeared, lost in our fucking.

Jace pushed in with a grunt and wrapped her hair around his fist. Then he yanked her head back and grazed his teeth along her neck. "Admit it, baby niece. You wanted your daddy and me to come in here and rape-fuck you."

"Yes!" she sobbed. "I'm sorry!"

I hissed, feeling every muscle in me flex.

It killed me to wait, but I didn't wanna come this way. I wanted to fuck her through the mattress before I filled her with my come, so I bided my time. I grasped Belle's face and kissed the tears away, then swallowed her pleas and sucked lightly on her tongue. She mewled and kissed me back possessively, and it hadn't escaped my notice that she was meeting Jace's thrusts.

"There's my little fuck doll," I murmured hoarsely.

"I-I don't know what's happening to m-me, Dad." She sniffled and acted as if she were trying to crawl under my skin. She let go of her bunny and clung to me. "Do I really feel good?"

"So good. Amazing." I kissed her deeply and twisted her nipples between my fingers. "You have the sweetest, tightest little pussy, and you've already got us addicted to you." I stifled a groan, not ready for my orgasm to start rolling yet. "Fuck... that's it, squeeze Daddy like that. Fuck yourself on me. You can be as greedy and slutty as you want with us."

"Every goddamn night." Jace picked up the pace and railed her ass, the tendons in his neck protruding. "Christ, almost there. Almost—*fuck.*"

When he finally came, I was close to losing it. Frustration had built up as rapidly as the need to come, and I watched him ride out his orgasm with my teeth gnashed so hard I feared I'd crush them.

Belle was gone. Moaning, crying, gasping, pleading incoherently.

My fucking turn.

In a burst of rage, I hauled her off of Jace and threw her onto her back next to me right as the final ropes of come shot out of his cock. He heaved a breath and stroked himself, easily positioning himself to milk the last of his release over Belle's breasts. In the meantime, I hooked an arm under her leg and rammed into her pussy.

I fucked her forcefully and fast, making sure my pelvis hit her clit on every thrust. She tried to wrap her arms around me, but she had no strength left, only able to make sounds of euphoric delirium. She didn't even seem to notice how the power behind my fucking was literally pushing her farther up the mattress.

The pressure increased inside me, bordering on painful with how I strained myself. I just couldn't slow down. The sounds of skin slapping and my cock pushing in and out of her drenched cunt sent me spiraling.

A fever broke out and made me flush.

My chest glistened. My jaw fucking hurt.

"Please, Daddy..." The breathiest whisper left her lips, and her eyes nearly rolled back. Then her mouth opened in a silent scream. She threw her head back and tightened impossibly around me.

Seeing her come was my undoing.

Everything erupted and unleashed inside me, and I slammed in once, twice more and surrendered to the climax. Bursts of come rushed up my shaft. I screwed my eyes shut and buried my face against her neck, rocking lazily into her pussy as I came.

Fuck.

I wasn't gonna be able to walk tomorrow.

Seconds passed, and with the fading high, the aches made themselves known. I pulled out of my girl, leaving a sodden mess behind, and collapsed in the middle of the bed.

Between the two exhausted sweethearts I called family.

Seven

"Stop squirming, darling."

"But you're touching me," she whined. "I want more."

"Not now." I kept my eyes on the flat screen and my hand between her legs. She was cuddled up across my lap, pitiful and adorable. She'd refused painkillers and a bath last night, which probably caused some of her aches to be worse today. Jace had made it his first task this morning instead, and he'd given her a bath while I made us breakfast. She'd taken a couple pills to relieve her soreness too, and I was rubbing some cooling lotion with aloe in it over her pussy.

It made her squirm.

I slid my fingers gently between her soft lips, over her clit, then down to her sore little opening.

"Daddy?"

"Hmm?"

"Where's Jace?" She tried to keep the breathiness out of her voice.

"Downstairs in the studio." He had final edits to go through so I could send his work on Patagonia to his agent. "He should be done soon."

"Okay. I'd like to talk to you later."

I flicked my gaze to her, concerned. "Is everything all right?"

She nodded and bit her lip. "I just...I don't want this to be all about sex."

There was no question what she was talking about. And as happy as I was to hear her say that, it raised concerns. I slipped my hand out from between her thighs and wiped the remainder of the lotion on the blanket covering her. Thinking about this was...strange. It did things to my chest. A flutter of hope, a rock of unease.

"For the record," I said, phrasing myself carefully, "this was never about just sex for me—or Jace, for that matter. But I'd like to hear your thoughts before I go on."

She straightened a bit and tucked the blanket under her arms. "Um, I guess what I mean is...c-can there be relation-shippy feelings and stuff also?" She blushed and looked down.

Fuck.

I took a breath and pressed my lips to her temple. Something inside me squeezed. I didn't want to think about the end of summer yet, and this conversation would catapult us right there.

"I want everything," I murmured. "But you're an incredible young woman, and you'll have to go easy on your old man. Because when you go back to London, I'll still be here. Jumping into a more serious relationship will make it even more difficult to be away from you."

She glanced up at that, questioning. "But you don't think it would be impossible to, you know, develop those feelings for me?"

I chuckled softly and stroked her cheek. "Belle, you and Jace are already my world. That's not because you're my daughter and he's my brother. I love you because of who you are as people. It's a million memories and all your quirks." I paused. "When I tell you I love you, I have all of that in the back of my mind. It's you when you were twelve and won that teddy bear at the fair—that big smile you wore. It's when you got into university and threw your arms around me..." And it was more than that too. "You're so smart, headstrong, and funny. Whether you're trying to teach me how to make your blueberry muffins or you're venting angrily about animal rights, I could listen to you for hours."

She ducked her head and buried her face in the crook of my neck. "Really?"

"Really." I kissed her shoulder. "All of this exists in every 'I love you.' Combined with chemistry and how inexplicably drawn I've become to you physically, I don't see how I have a choice but to keep loving you more and more for every day, in old ways and new."

She hugged my neck tightly.

"Same here."

It wasn't Belle who'd spoken. We both looked behind us to find Jace leaning against the wide doorway to the kitchen.

"I think I speak for both Andrew and me when I say we wanna explore other shit too." He walked over and kissed the top of Belle's head. "Dates, this dynamic, the future, you name it."

I nodded and nudged up Belle's chin. "What I'm suggesting is we dive in as soon as you get your cute bottom back from England."

"We're already gonna be miserable fucks when you leave." Jace smirked at her. "No need to make it worse, right?"

She was thinking hard on something. I'd known her for so

long that I recognized every expression and what it meant. Brow furrowed, mouth twisted sideways, gaze flicking.

"Hey." Jace gave my shoulder a little squeeze. "Did you talk to her about...? You know."

That derailed Belle's thoughts, and she perked up curiously.

I shook my head in response. "Not yet." Partly because I didn't fucking want to.

Jace had raised the issue with me earlier, about whether or not Belle was on birth control. I couldn't recall that she was, and the images my brother had unknowingly forced into my head were wreaking havoc.

Small as it was, there was a chance I'd impregnated Belle last night, and I couldn't for the life of me think of anything more extraordinary. It filled me with a possessiveness that bordered on savage, and I wanted to do it again and again and again.

"Is something wrong?" Belle asked.

"No, baby," Jace replied.

"It's about protection," I admitted. Underneath the blanket, my hand went to her stomach. Just that little gesture caused my cock to stir. "We're certainly clean, but there's the matter of birth control."

"Oh," she whispered. Her eyes widened at the realization of what this meant, and she looked down and put her hands over mine. "Crap, I didn't think."

"You're literally the last person we'd blame," Jace said with a wry quirk of his lips.

I agreed with him. "This is on me, darling. I should have used a condom."

Belle's dismayed expression mirrored what I felt, but she probably wasn't thinking about the ramifications yet. I knew she loved kids, as did I. That wasn't the issue. An ill-timed pregnancy would get in the way of her education.

I couldn't allow that. *She* couldn't allow that. She loved school too.

"Dad..." Belle affected a shy look and burrowed herself closer. "There's a chance you put a baby in me last night."

"Jesus fucking Christ," I whispered.

"The mouth on you, girl," Jace groaned.

Belle straddled me, blushing furiously but seemingly on a mission. "I have this fantasy. Of you two taking turns—" She was stopped—a damn good thing—by Jace, who leaned over and grabbed her jaw firmly.

"Think twice before you speak again," he told her. He inched closer until his lips brushed hers. He was stronger than I was. I couldn't argue with her, not about this. My hands were gripping her hips, and my cock was officially rock-solid.

"Listen to me," she pleaded, still in Jace's grasp. "You would make amazing fathers." I cursed as she tried to roll her hips over my erection. The only clothes she wore—panties and some flimsy little top—would be so easily ripped off her. "And think about how wild this could get. By night...Daddy and Uncle breed their little girl—"

"You're fucking obscene," Jace hissed and let go of her jaw.

I was going to crush my molars if I gnashed my teeth any harder. "This is serious."

She bit her lip and slid her gaze to me. "If we had a baby, you'd be Grandpa also." She made my heart stop. The filthy little whore was putting these fantasies in my head; it was her goddamn doing. "That would be between just us three, but..." She shimmied her delectable body over my cock, and I grunted under my breath. "The hottest, dirtiest Grandpa who visits me at night—"

"That's enough, Belle," I growled. She was going to be the actual death of me. "Life is not a fantasy."

Jace was caving, trailing kisses along her neck, and I needed him on my side. "We should use condoms," he rasped unconvincingly. "There will be time for all that other shit when you come home from school."

"He's right," I said firmly. "I'll go buy protection today."

Belle pouted.

Eight

We were responsible from that day on. Well, for the most part.

Occasionally.

For the next two weeks, we did little else but fuck, eat, watch movies, sleep, and fuck more. Belle canceled plans with her friends, Jace barely went down to the studio, and I all but forgot the stock market existed.

My room had turned into everyone's bedroom, and at least one of us always had wandering hands. Belle was an insatiable nymph, and she'd created monsters out of Jace and me. Every morning started out the same. I woke up with a thirsty little mouth on my cock, and once I came down Belle's throat, she crawled over to Jace who was ready to give her a good-morning fuck.

They were usually done by the time I'd made us breakfast, after which we migrated to the roof if the weather allowed it.

That was where Belle had made us cave and forego protection the first time. Pool sex. We couldn't use condoms in the water.

I liked to think we'd put up a good fight, but...

I shook my head to myself and stepped out of the shower. Jace was making lunch, so it was probably best I checked in on him before he burned down the kitchen. Wrapping a towel around my hips, I left the bathroom while running another towel over my head.

Well, at least he wasn't setting anything on fire. He was literally staring at a pot of water. Correction, he was waiting for pasta to boil.

"This is about as fun as watching paint dry," he said. "I can't believe you like this cooking shit."

I chuckled and draped the towel around my neck. "What's Belle doing?"

"Last I saw, she was reading a book in the pool."

"The one she borrowed from me?" I'd been pleasantly surprised when I saw the book on third world economics on her nightstand. I knew she was trying to get familiar with our hobbies, and I thought that was sweet of her. She didn't have to enjoy the world of finance, but it meant a great deal that she made even the slightest effort.

"I wouldn't know." He peered into the pot on the stove. "She was topless."

I rolled my eyes and opened the fridge. "For chrissakes, Jace." Given the lack of food on the counter, it looked like we'd be eating nothing but pasta. So I grabbed a container of leftover chicken, a carton of cream, what little left we had of the cream cheese, and a block of parmesan. "She's more than a body, you know."

"Don't give me that." He snorted. "You fell asleep last night when she and I talked."

He had me there. And I wouldn't say they "talked." They

debated heatedly—about something happening in Asia or... whatnot. It'd been a complete snoozefest for me.

"I'm addicted to the girl, Andrew." He looked almost worried about it. "She speaks and I automatically push everything else to the side. I'm only like that with you—but you know...differently."

I couldn't help but smile at that, and I gave his neck an affectionate squeeze. "You're falling for her, little brother. I've seen you."

I'd seen him with previous girlfriends. I'd seen him with friends. This was entirely different. And it was magnificent to watch.

Emptying the container with three chicken breasts onto a thick cutting board, I picked out a knife and started slicing the pieces into thin strips.

"And in a couple weeks, she's gone again."

I set down the knife and took a long breath, despising the topic. "We'll visit." Because I wouldn't be able to settle for Skype this time. "She'll be home permanently in a year."

"I know," he replied quietly. I handed him a wooden spoon to stir the pasta. "It's not just for her, you know. We've always had it good, you and me, but..."

I nodded. He and I had grown closer this summer as well— not in the biblical sense where we happened to share a bed with a lovely young woman—but our relationship as brothers. Our roles had become clearer, and our bond was stronger.

Abandoning the chicken, I drew him in for a tight hug. "She won't get rid of us."

"She better not." He hugged my midsection and rested his forehead on my shoulder. "Why didn't this happen next year?"

I smirked and gave his temple a kiss before letting go. "At least you'll have your travels this fall. I'll be stuck here alone."

He'd have a month in Canada, two weeks in northern California, and then three weeks right here in Washington. I'd booked a gig for him in the peninsula, and it didn't get more local than that. Although, despite the close proximity, he'd be out of range until he reemerged from the forest to check in with his fretting brother.

Perhaps we could visit Belle over the holidays and spend Christmas in London. I'd need it after being away from both of them.

"Your Alfredo is the *best*, Dad." Belle reached over and popped a kiss to my shoulder. I winked at her. "Can I have some more wine, please?"

Jace refilled her glass while I leaned back in my chair and closed my eyes, face tilted toward the sun. I hadn't bothered putting on clothes, content with the towel around my hips. We'd been lucky with the weather this week, and my body was soaking up all the sunlight it possibly could.

I listened with one ear as Belle and Jace chatted about her future plans. He mentioned his college friend, Casey, whose partner ran a PR agency in town, and Belle said it'd be a dream to work there. Apparently, the owner was well-known on the West Coast for those who knew a thing or two about marketing.

Local was good. It was all I cared about—and that she would be happy with her job.

They continued discussing work, and I drifted, more content than ever. The sun was perfect, the voices of my two loved ones were like music to my ears, and the afternoon glass of wine was settling in.

The future looked bright. I only had to make it through one more year.

A whole goddamn year.

These past two weeks had shown me so much. Or perhaps it'd been there for a while, but now my eyes were opened. Figuratively.

Belle's sweet giggles and Jace's soft laughter would never get old. Or how they interacted. Just the other week, she'd sauntered out of her room in some preppy getup and a pair of black-framed glasses. She'd looked admittedly sinful, and she'd told me Jace had a librarian fantasy. And unless he gave up the rights to the remote control, she wasn't going to fulfill his dreams.

Of course, he'd chased her down like a man possessed and fucked her on the hallway floor, so I supposed the last laugh had been his.

I couldn't recall sex ever being this thrilling, and I had every intention of taking advantage as often as I could until it was time to drive Belle to the airport.

My hunger for her only grew. The more I fucked her, the more I needed her. On the kitchen counter, on the couch, in the shower, in a goddamn dressing room...

"Not here, Dad!" she hissed.

"Yes. Here, baby." I unzipped my pants. "This is what you get for teasing me. Lift your skirt. If you're quiet, I'll buy it for you."

A few seconds later, I had a hand clamped over her mouth and was fucking her up against the mirror. I watched her fight the pleasure, her scowl weakening until the desire took over completely and her eyes swam with need.

"Harder," she whimpered.

"You're a little cock addict, aren't you?" I tried to control my breathing, and I hiked my free arm under her leg to angle her better. "That's it, deeper. Beg for your father's come."

She gasped and tightened around my cock. "Please, Daddy. Fill me."

Breed her. You want it.

I screwed my eyes shut and pumped into her faster.

In the underground garage at home...

One minute, she was cleaning up the wet spot she'd left on the passenger's seat, and when she was bent over that perfectly, I couldn't help myself. I pushed down her leggings and fucked her from behind while our groceries sat on the ground.

Her breathless moans echoed, fueling me.

"Someone can come any minute," she whined.

"I'll need a few more than that." I grunted and gripped her hips tightly. "You have a perfect little cunt, darling. Daddy can't resist, you know that."

Fill her, fill her, fill her.

"Fuck," I growled.

After her bath...

I got down on one knee and rubbed her dry with the towel. Higher up, the insides of her thighs. My knuckles ghosted over her soft pussy lips, causing my mouth to water. Belle shivered and looked down at me with an increasingly familiar expression. My baby wanted.

"You like it when Daddy kisses you here?" I brushed the pad of my thumb between the lips and circled her clit softly.

She nodded and stuck her thumb into her mouth, and *that* sight... I groaned and leaned in, licking her cunt greedily.

Jace entered the bathroom to shower, but seeing him gave me a better idea. So I picked Belle up and sat her on the bathroom counter. Then I urged Jace closer and told him to give it to her quickly. Standing behind him, I helped him with his jeans while he leaned over her and kissed her passionately.

He was hard and ready, and I gripped the base of his cock. I teased her soaked pussy with the head of him.

"*Please*," Belle moaned.

"Fuck her," I whispered. "She's not leaving this bathroom until her little tummy is full of come."

Jace gave me a sharp look.

I stared right back and slowly pushed him inside her. "Breed your niece. You want it."

A shudder ripped through him, and he faced forward.

While he fucked her, I stood to the side and stroked my cock. Their grunts and groans bounced off the walls, and I was ready to burst by the time Jace rocked into her and came with a guttural moan.

It was my turn then, and I got between her legs, only to glide through the mess Jace had left in her and empty myself as Belle convulsed around me.

In bed...

"I can't come again," she whimpered.

"I think you can." I tasted the drop of perspiration trickling down her neck, and Jace and I continued to finger her pussy. On her back in the middle of the bed, with us on each side of her, she had her legs hitched over our thighs. Our hands traveled along her body, stroking and rubbing and pinching.

Jace pushed two fingers inside her while I rubbed our

previous releases over her clit. Her little cunt was soaked in come and her own juices.

She gasped.

"You liked that," Jace murmured. "Right there?"

She nodded and nodded and nodded and begged. I swiped my thumb over her sensitive clit and applied pressure. At the same time, her mouth called to me, and we met in a fiery kiss. Jace trailed the tip of his tongue up the slope of her neck until he joined us. I tasted delicious sex on both of them, and it sent another spike of desire through me.

I didn't know how it was possible. We'd been making love all day. My body was tired and protesting, yet I couldn't get enough of being with them like this.

"I need her again," Jace croaked.

"Take her." I nipped at his bottom lip before stealing a hungry kiss from Belle. "I'll go next."

"Oh my God," Belle moaned breathlessly.

As Jace crawled over her and shoved his cock inside her, I cupped her breast and sucked a nipple into my mouth. Her fingers disappeared into my hair while she cried out for her daddy and uncle and how much she needed us.

I caressed her soft stomach, picturing it growing with a child, and I groaned into the next kiss. "The day we make you pregnant, little girl, we'll never let you out of our sight."

"Not a chance," Jace breathed. "Fuck. We should stretch her pussy to fit both of us. No more taking turns to fill her womb."

"What do you think about that?" I brushed some hair away from her cheek, and I could tell she was as intrigued as she was scared by the idea. "Do you think we could stretch your little baby pussy to take two cocks?"

She stiffened just as Jace let out a breathless laugh.

"Her cunt approves," he grunted. "A more come-hungry slut hole's gotta be impossible to find."

"Not today," Belle pleaded.

"Not today," I agreed. Moving a hand farther down, I played with her clit and spread her lips that were already stretched around Jace's cock. "One day."

She nodded and nuzzled my cheek. "After lots and lots of preparation, Daddy."

"We'll prepare you just fine."

Jace came with a moan, and I gave my cock a few strokes, ready to take over.

Nine

Three days before Belle was set to return to London, our bubble was mildly burst by a friend of mine who said it was time to stop avoiding reality.

"You've been holed up all summer, my friend. Let's meet up for a drink, at least."

I agreed, not because he was right, but because Belle and Jace wanted to go dancing. Camassia clubs weren't big. Some fifty people filled the dance floor, yet I'd already lost sight of Belle and my brother. But they were enjoying themselves, and that was all that mattered. And, I had to admit, it was nice to get out of the loft for one evening.

"I still don't see your problem, Andrew." Alex took a swig of his whiskey, and we found an empty table and two low leather chairs in the back. The seating area was located on a platform that made it easier to see the people dancing.

I spotted Jace first, then a mane of pink hair, thanks to the spotlights traveling across the crowd.

"Possibly because you're already a deviant." I smirked at my friend and set my drink on the table. "You know as well as I do that we're going to face some sort of backlash due to the nature of our relationship."

He looked out pensively at the people dancing. "You'll come out as a triad. There are plenty of those."

"They're usually not related, Alex," I pointed out. "It doesn't matter how appropriate the relationship is between Jace and me. People will see us as brothers—because we are."

He nodded slowly and set down his drink. "Fair enough. There will probably be some...issues. But I don't think they'll affect you long term."

I hoped he was right. Thankfully, my circle of friends was small, and there was no family to speak of. Belle would face the biggest backlash from peers who found it gross, though she seemed incredibly unperturbed. *"So I'll make new friends,"* she'd said. *"Life's too short, Dad."*

My God, how I loved her. My chest swelled up and tightened as I saw her goofing around with Jace on the floor. I adored being her father—almost as much as I loved being one of her men.

I wanted it to stay that way. We'd discussed it, albeit briefly, and agreed that we had to keep certain aspects private. It was simply easier and more comfortable that way. But between the three of us, there were several natural roles to shoulder, and they all mattered in one way or another.

"You're in love with her," Alex noted.

I looked away from Belle and Jace and grabbed my drink. "If I'm not, I'm certainly almost there. She's my world. Jace too."

"So focus on that." He leaned forward and held up his glass. "Fuck what the rest of the world thinks."

I nodded and clinked my glass to his. "Indeed. Cheers, buddy." I took a swallow and enjoyed the smooth, smoky burn of the drink. "Enough about me. How's life in your own kinky world?"

Alex was involved in BDSM, and last I'd heard, he'd hired a submissive slash escort to tend to both his house and his needs. At least, that was how he'd described it, along with a slight grimace and admission that it was a simplification of things.

"I suppose I got more than I bargained for." He peered into his glass, swirling the liquid. "Let's just say you and I might have more in common than you think."

"Or you can say more than that," I told him. I'd confided in him; he could ease his burden by confiding in me. He was only a few years older than me. Not an excuse to suddenly look as if he were ready for retirement age.

Alex sighed, the sound drowned out by the music, and finished his drink in one go. "She's lying to me. Lola." The girl he'd hired. "I told her she and I were to be exclusive—for health purposes." That made sense. "Now I've found out she has a boyfriend, and he knows about me."

I winced, sympathetic. Not many years ago, Alex's fiancée cheated on him. More than that, it was revealed that the child she was carrying wasn't his. He'd been devastated for a long time.

"Have you confronted her?" I asked.

He shook his head. "Not yet." And it was clear why. The friend I'd known for years, who had sworn off women and acted quite cold toward them—for obvious reasons—had developed feelings for this one. "It gets worse." He smirked wryly. "I assume she and her boyfriend are polyamorous, because he's hooking up with my little brother."

"*Jesus.* Which one?" I'd met all three of them. Adam, in particular, who ran our favorite steakhouse.

"Jamie," Alex replied. "He doesn't know any of this."

Ah, the youngest brother, and they happened to live

together...wait. I cocked my head. "Didn't you tell me he was struggling with the feelings he had for his ex-girlfriend's daughter?"

"Yeah..." He chuckled and looked away. "Makes you feel a little better about your own situation, doesn't it?"

"A bit." Or a lot, because sweet Jesus, I'd already lost track of who was fucking whom in Alex's story. On a more serious note, he should've come to me sooner. "Alex, I may have perfected the part of a hermit this summer, but you know you can call me whenever, yes?"

"I do." He nodded. "I appreciate it. It kind of snowballed this week. Before then, I thought everything was okay."

No wonder he felt the need to forget things for one evening.

"Well, next drink is on me—" I was cut off by the sound of Belle's laughter, and it alerted me to the fact that she and Jace were coming over.

"Hi, silver foxes," she giggled and plopped down in my lap. Jace had clearly bought her a couple drinks already.

"Hello, little one." Alex smiled indulgently at her. "You enjoying yourself?"

She nodded vigorously, and Jace sat down on the armrest of my chair. "Daddy says you know about our dynamic and that you're okay with it."

I smiled and tucked a piece of hair behind her ear.

"Of course I am," Alex chuckled. "It's what makes you happy, isn't it?" Another nod from Belle. "Then, as a friend, that's enough for me."

Jace scratched my neck with a finger, and I peered up at him in question. But he wasn't looking at me. He was merely smiling to himself as Alex and Belle chatted, and the little gesture meant a lot to me. This wasn't Belle and me and Belle and Jace. It was the three of us together as a unit, and in one way or another, we were more freely showing affection just for the sake of it.

It gave me enough hope that we'd pull through this last year before Belle returned to us for good. It was going to be difficult, but we had a lot to fight for.

EPILOGUE *One*

BELLE'S SURPRISE

A couple months later

"In fact, here he is right now. Bennett, a minute, please."

I followed his gaze and looked out over the bullpen. A man had recently stepped out of the elevator, and he rounded the area where some ten or eleven people were working.

"Yes, sir?" The man, Bennett, was handsome and had a charismatic smile. He looked to be around Jace's age.

Jace. I miss him.

My new boss, on the other hand, was a little older and had the same warmth to him as Daddy.

Ugh. I missed him too. So, so much.

"I want you to meet Belle Hart, your new intern," my boss introduced. "Belle, this is Bennett Brooks. He's an account exec here."

"Pleased to meet you, Ms. Hart." Bennett's English accent was more rounded than what I was used to. Americanized for sure.

I shook his hand and hoped I didn't mess this up because of my nerves. "Yes, sir. I mean likewise." Motherfucker. "I'm sorry. I read about your work with Westwater Hotels, and I'm a little excited."

He chuckled. "Welcome on board, then." He shifted his gaze back to my boss. Although, technically, I guessed they were both my bosses now. "I'll put her with Meghan if you don't mind."

"Sounds good." Mr. Hayes inclined his head. "I have a lunch meeting, so I'll be off. Belle, happy to have you here. You're in good hands with Bennett and Meghan."

"Thank you again for this opportunity, sir." I shook his hand, more grateful than I could say. I'd taken a chance when contacting him to explain my situation, and most wouldn't even have replied. It wasn't his job to hire interns, nor was I a particularly good investment at the moment, yet he'd been so nice to me.

Things were falling into place. I couldn't believe my luck.

An hour later, Meghan—a funny, lovely woman—had shown me around the agency, and I'd been given a preliminary schedule for when I started next week. Returning to my room, I checked in with the delivery guys who were probably sick of me calling to make sure everything would arrive on time.

They assured me it would.

That left only one thing, and I looked at my watch. Daddy and Jace should both be home. Jace was probably tired. He'd just spent two weeks in the mountains taking some breathtaking photos for a travel magazine. Now he had a week of editing before going off again, so there was no time to waste.

I checked out of the inn with my one roll-aboard and thanked the woman for ordering me a taxi.

It was only a five-minute drive, but cobblestones sucked when you had luggage on wheels, and I was jet-lagged. It was my excuse, and I was sticking to it.

Butterflies fluttered in my stomach as I stepped out of the taxi right outside Jace's studio. The front room was dark, and I knew it was closed. Though, it was possible Daddy was in his office in the back.

I could barely contain my grin as I pulled out my phone. Then I called Daddy on Skype and dragged my luggage closer to the house wall. I didn't want my background to give away my location just yet.

He answered on the second ring.

"Hi!" I beamed at his gorgeous face.

His features softened, and he smiled into the camera. "Hello, my beautiful girl. I take it you have good news?"

I nodded. "I got the internship!" Only, he thought it was in England. "I'll start next week. I'm so excited."

His grin said it all. He put my happiness first and was relieved for my sake. For his own sake, this was a blow. It was one of the reasons I loved him so much. And therefore, it was my mission to put *him* first. Him and Jace.

On the other hand, I wasn't sacrificing a damn thing here. The only reason I'd wanted to study in England in the first place was to get as far away as possible from the temptation of Daddy and Jace, and it was time to tell them that.

First, I finished my prattling about the internship. For six months, I'd shadow some pretty fucking cool men and women in marketing, and sure, I'd probably fetch a lot of coffee too. Daddy chuckled at that bit. *My Andrew*. God, I couldn't stop staring at him. I missed them to the point where my body was screaming.

Last night when I'd texted a little with Jace, I'd almost told him I was a few blocks away at a bed-and-breakfast. But I'd wanted everything ready before I told them. And now it was. I had my internship, my stuff from London was arriving in a couple hours, and...I was home.

"So, where's Jace?" I asked.

"He's..." He looked over his phone. I wasn't sure, but I thought he was in the living room. On the couch. It wouldn't surprise me if the coffee table were littered with finance sections from the three papers he subscribed to. As if they reported different numbers. "Here he is. Belle's on the phone."

Yup, he was on the couch, and I heard paper rustling. Then Jace plopped down beside Daddy, all wet and sinful-looking. He'd just come out of the shower.

"Hi, baby." Jace smirked.

"Hi, hot stuff." I bit my lip, 'cause this was it. "So, I wanted to tell you guys something." I waited while a couple ladies passed me on the sidewalk. "You already know I wanted this to happen between us for, like, forever. But I haven't told you it's the reason I wanted to study out of the country." My smile turned nervous as they wore matching frowns of concern. I shrugged a little. "I thought, if I put distance between us, I'd get over my feelings. But, of course, I didn't, and now we're together."

Jace looked to Daddy. "Is she saying what I think she's saying?"

"Don't jinx us," was Daddy's quick reply. "Go on, darling."

I giggled, fucking giddy. "I should probably mention that the internship I got is at the Three Dots Agency here in town."

"Holy fuck," Jace blurted.

"So...do you wanna come down and help me with my luggage?" I asked sweetly.

Jace reacted the fastest, disappearing from the screen in a blur.

"Are you truly—" Daddy shook his head, dazed. "Don't move. We'll be right there. *Don't move.*"

The call was disconnected, and my face hurt from smiling.

Less than a minute later, Jace stumbled out of the door, barefoot and bare-chested, still zipping up his jeans. And Daddy was right behind him, and then I was engulfed by them.

I was home.

In between kisses and the best hugs, I was bombarded with questions. How long had I been here, why didn't I call, was I really home to stay, what about school—the list went on. I managed to answer most of them, mainly that I'd transferred my studies to Seattle, which was less than two hours away.

"But that will wait," I said, snuggling into Daddy's chest.

"Six months of interning first," Jace concluded with a nod.

I popped a kiss to his chin and smiled. "Plus another year off, I think. I can't very well pick up my studies right around my due date—"

"*Belle.*" Daddy stared me down, shocked.

Jace's own wide-eyed gaze dropped to my stomach.

"Yeah..." I stifled a squeal, having wanted to see their reactions for a week now. "One of you totally knocked me up this summer."

EPILOGUE *Two*

DADDY JACE

A few years later

"There's cell service now."

"Cool, thanks." I sidestepped a fern and patted down the multiple pockets in my camos. After two weeks in the forests of the Alaskan peninsula, I was itching for a piece of civilization. More than that, I fucking ached for my family.

My company during this gig had been stellar, though, and both Kyle and Logan were my new go-tos for work I did in Alaska. They were a married couple and knew an annoyingly high amount about the wilderness. From hunting and fishing to tracking and safety. They were resourceful as fuck and made me look like an amateur, and I'd been running around in the woods since I could walk.

I was coming home with some amazing images, not to

mention memories. Kyle had managed to take me into the heart of a growing wolf pack. If my editor was interested, I wanted to come back in a year to track the pups' progress.

"Is it bad that I hope the twins are potty-trained by now?" I asked, scrolling through my Facebook feed.

Kyle snorted.

"We've been gone two weeks, not two months," Logan chuckled.

"You haven't met Belle." I grinned at the pictures Belle had uploaded of the kids and turned one of them into my lock screen. Max was fiercely protective of his baby brothers, which I suspected would get ten times worse when our first—and last —daughter was born. We'd *thought* the twins would be the last, but...well, our track record of using rubbers wasn't the best.

Four was a fucking great number, though.

So was fifteen, I thought, as I checked the number of people who'd RSVP'd to my birthday dinner next week. I was turning thirty-five, and according to Andrew, we should go all out. With this being our last year in the loft before we moved to a bigger house, we hosted quite a few dinner parties on the roof. Andrew was planning this one and had promised catering from our favorite steakhouse.

"Trail's ahead," Kyle announced.

I looked up and exhaled. First sign of civilization, a dirt road. Then I'd suffer a ride in Kyle's bush plane to Anchorage, and from there, fly to Seattle. Where I fucking hoped Andrew would pick me up.

"Thirty-six hours till I get laid." I adjusted my backpack. "Thirty-six hours till the last sounds of fucking aren't coming from you two."

Logan grinned and looked away, slightly more modest than his hubby.

Kyle lifted a brow and smirked. "Kept the bears away, didn't it?"

I rolled my eyes, chuckling.

When we reached the trail, I gained my bearings a bit more and remembered certain things. The hunting lodge would be at the center of a clearing that was coming up next. There would be a fallen tree covered in fungi and a carved-out tree stump that'd been used as a grill. Another twenty minutes toward the edge of the forest, there was a small parking lot. Only four-wheelers were allowed on this dirt road, and the land was private. At least, I thought we'd reached the private property of Kyle and Logan's company.

"I think you can call Justin," Kyle said to Logan, referring to their son. He taught tourist kids how to safely drive ATVs around here. "If the coffee's not on when we get to the cabin, he's grounded."

I smiled and wiped my forehead. It was beginning to drizzle, though the sun made appearances here and there.

I looked forward to a hot meal and to sit my ass down on the porch for a couple hours. Hopefully, the reception would be good enough for me to Skype with my kids too.

"Listen." Logan cocked his head, having picked up on a sound. It was something I'd discovered quickly. They *heard* goddamn everything. I heard birds chirping. "Maybe he booked a class. I hear children."

It wasn't until we passed the fungi tree right before the clearing that I heard said children, and now it was my turn to pay extra attention. "Uh..." The boy laughing sounded weirdly fucking familiar. It was followed by the soft, unmistakable laughter of my girl.

They're here.

The excitement that tore through me was unlike anything else, and I jogged into the clearing and felt my face splitting into a grin. Holy shit, they'd come all the way up here to see me. Andrew was sitting on the porch steps with one of the twins, teaching him how to work a bow and arrow. Belle was running around in the clearing with our other two, plus three dogs that I knew belonged to Kyle and Logan.

Max was the first to spot me. "Daddy!" His shout bounced between the trees and alerted everyone else to our arrival. "We're surprising you!"

I laughed and unbuckled the strap to my backpack. "Color me fucking shocked. Get the hell over here." He started running, and I dropped the backpack on the ground right before I caught him. "Did you miss me as much as I missed you?"

"Yeah, and I got a new skateboard!"

I grinned and smooched his face. He'd recently lost his baby chubbiness, and I wasn't too happy about that. "You'll have to show me when we get home." By then, the twins and the dogs surrounded me, and I was lost to them for several minutes. The twins spoke rapidly about everything they'd done while I was gone. I did my best to keep up with the toddler speak. Mommy wasn't sick in the morning anymore, Dad had burned his finger on the stove, Daddy *sucked* at answering the phone—

"Remember what I said, buddy?" I adjusted David's beanie. "I can't use the phone in the woods."

He nodded. "Sucks! You take pics for Mommy's Istagwam?"

"Instagram," I corrected with a soft laugh. "Sure, I took loads of pictures for her. That's why I do this. So she can post them online."

He looked over his shoulder, toward Belle and Andrew, who walked toward us hand in hand. *Fuck*, she was beautiful. "Mommy, he took pics!"

"That's 'cause he's a good daddy." Belle winked. As soon as she was within reach, I pulled her in for a hard kiss. She'd gained a few pounds, not that I'd ever tell her that, and she was showing more and more. Every pregnancy was the same. I turned into a starving lunatic the minute she gained some baby weight, and I was secretly thrilled she didn't lose every single pound after the birth.

Okay, it was a secret I shared with Andrew.

As the kids and the dogs scattered, it was just Belle, Andrew, and me.

"Best surprise in a long time, love." I kissed the smile off her perfect face and threaded our fingers together. "Our baby girl treatin' you okay?"

"She's an angel compared to the other heathens." She patted her belly, humor evident in her green eyes. "I think this one will finally take after me."

Andrew and I exchanged a look.

"Then we're all fucking screwed," I told her.

She thought that was funny.

With a shake of my head, I faced my brother and hugged him too.

"I heard you burned your finger."

He scoffed. "Did David snitch on me? I tried to make Belle's blueberry muffins again."

I laughed under my breath and pressed a kiss to his shoulder, to which he draped an arm around me and pulled me close.

"David!" he called, and our son looked up from whatever he was playing with in the grass. "Son, I thought we agreed to keep the stove incident to ourselves?"

David shrugged and scrunched his nose. "I forgotted things, Dad. Can I have ice cweam now?"

"Guess my answer," Andrew grumbled quietly.

"You poor thing." Belle mock-pouted at him.

I merely looked at her as she teased Andrew, and I didn't know how it was possible to love her more than I already did.

Yet, time and time again, she proved me wrong and made me fall a little harder.

"Okay, let's get Jace off his feet for a bit," she said. "You look tired, honey."

"Thanks." I threw her a smirk.

"You know what I mean, dork." She giggled and slipped under my arm, and I kissed her temple. "We wanna hear everything about your trip."

"You must be hungry," Andrew added. "We brought food for everyone from Anchorage."

"I'm *starving*."

Most of all, for them.

The sweet and dirty hearts of my life.

MORE FROM CARA DEE

In Camassia Cove, everyone has a story to share
Alex
Casey
Bennett
With a special glimpse of Logan and Kyle from Northland

IF YOU ENJOYED THIS BOOK,
YOU MIGHT LIKE THE FOLLOWING.

Forbidden Gem (M/F) Gemma...she was once sweeter than sugar. Now she's sweeter than sin, and she's also the estranged stepdaughter Dean did not expect to find at his cabin when he arrives for his annual month of peace and quiet.

Power Play (M/M) Abel has always loved Madigan, one of his parents' closest friends, but being near Madigan has become too painful. That's the thing about unrequited love—it hurts. And now Abel has to suck it up for the two weeks he's home. He has to pretend everything is okay, though there is one man who doesn't buy the act. A jaded tattoo artist and Daddy Dom named Madigan Monroe.

Touch: The Complete Series (M/F, M/M/F) Everyone's getting their kink on in San Francisco. This is the complete series, consisting of seven novellas and novels, several outtakes and future takes, about men and women finding their way in BDSM. Heavy on Daddykink and other fetishes.

Check out Cara's entire collection at www.caradeewrites.com, and don't forget to sign up for her newsletter so you don't miss any new releases, updates on book signings, giveaways, and much more.

ABOUT CARA DEE

I'm often awkwardly silent or, if the topic interests me, a chronic rambler. In other words, I can discuss writing forever and ever. Fiction, in particular. The love story—while a huge draw and constantly present—is secondary for me, because there's so much more to writing romance fiction than just making two (or more) people fall in love and have hot sex. There's a world to build, characters to develop, interests to create, and a topic or two to research thoroughly. Every book is a challenge for me, an opportunity to learn something new, and a puzzle to piece together. I want my characters to come to life, and the only way I know to do that is to give them substance—passions, history, goals, quirks, and strong opinions—and to let them evolve. Additionally, I want my men and women to be relatable. That means allowing room for everyday problems and, for lack of a better word, flaws. My characters will never be perfect.

Wait...this was supposed to be about me, not my writing.

I'm a writey person who loves to write. Always wanderlusting, twitterpating, kinking, and geeking. There's time for hockey and cupcakes, too. But mostly, I just love to write.

~Cara.

Made in the USA
Middletown, DE
01 May 2018